New Hope City

SUNHI MISTWALKER

New Hope City
By SunHi Mistwalker
Copyright © 2012
http://www.sunhimistwalker.com

Published by Dark Tales Great Lives, LLC

ISBN-10: 0984663622
ISBN-13: 978-0-9846636-2-0

Cover art created by Keri Knutson

Chapter 1

Only ten years ago, a fresh faced young man or woman knew that Hwy 582 was the road to a new promised land, a place called New Hope City that had a wealth of glittery skyscrapers, slick new housing developments and enough jobs to employ the whole entire country. Or, at least that's how the legend went. They would drive right down Hwy 582 passing more than a dozen towns whose dimmed city lights and hollowed residential developments told a tale of epic failure. But the newcomers looked neither right, nor left. They also never looked behind at the ravages of the rolling crash. They only had eyes for the promised land which sat like a shining jewel right off Exit 35, untouched by the chaos which was quickly engulfing the nation. And it was true for awhile, for what seemed like a golden era, that anyone who could make it to New Hope City could make it in life and escape the fate of their fallen brothers and sisters who stayed behind — wherever behind happened to be. Those "left behind" suffered terribly from rising crime which often escalated to small scale wars waged with the blessing of corrupt city officials, but paid for with the lives of citizens. Those left behind lost jobs, lost houses, lost their small rented rooms over someone's garage and they even lost the dingy lean-to shacks they paid for by doing things — jobs they thought they would never do, that they hoped they would never have to do. If only they had come to New Hope City their lives would have been spared, no, more than spared — improved by vast amounts, at least for a brief time. For it didn't take long to see the cracks in New Hope's beautiful façade. Not that the city was a beautiful liar who deceived those who were seduced by her charms, that wasn't it at all. She in fact was honest, an honest host, more honest than now, definitely. It was those who came with dreams and fears and aspirations that they thrust upon her shoulders, shoulders that were truly no wider than any other city but that just happened to be adorned with all the décor hopeful men and women looked for when searching for a savior. The most devout believers could not see the beginning of the end. Even when the skyscrapers emptied out five years ago and the lights dimmed like the other failed cities, New Hope's most devoted believers could not see what was right before their eyes. It was only when the nation's currency became more worthless than a child's play money and the organized gangs tried to take hold of the city center that even the most blind of them accepted that the great rolling crash had reached New Hope's safe shores. And the strangest thing was that it was the most devoted who were the quickest to leave once they realized that their savior's shoulders had given out. A great shift occurred, a change of powers and now everything is different. The once swank and bourgeoisie downtown enclave has been pillaged, it's inhabitants up and moved to the furthermost northern edge of the city, wedged between the city's last remaining church and it's burgeoning slums in the south where the poorest residents struggle to eke out a living. The poorest workers live in trailers which are nothing more than metal shacks that haven't seen maintenance in years. It is here where only the illusion of law and order exists and it is here where so many people of New Hope suffer the most.

Chapter 2

Long black hair flows behind the thin frame of a teenage girl. As her tattered sneakers slam into the slush covered road, her jeans become sullied with mud. She pumps her fists harder as she tries to run faster, her worn leather satchel hammering against her hip. The boys close in on her. There are six of them. They are fast. But the fastest, a freckled face boy with blond hair, quickly closes the distance. He reaches out to grab her. She can feel his talon-like fingernails stab at her shoulder. She pumps her arms harder and digs her sneakers into the mud in earnest. Panting heavily, sweat soaking her brow, she comes to a chain linked fence on the edge of the trailer park; but there is no exit, no way to get through. She claws at the fence trying to scale it; but the blond boy's talons hook onto the hood of her jacket and yank her to the ground. Not more than a few seconds pass before the other boys swarm Sunni as she lies in a dirty mix of mud and snow. Baine lifts his talons, palm jutted out towards his pack of fellow hunters, "Back the fuck off!" The other boys stop, back up, but only slightly, just enough to allow Baine room to bend over and relieve Sunni of her leather satchel and dump its contents onto the ground. Four tins of sardines, a box of saltine crackers and a pair of tiny pink ballerina shoes pour out of the bag and onto the slush covered pavement.

Sunni drags herself backwards and presses her spine into the fence. Her lips mold into a snarl; but she keeps her angry gaze hidden. The sound of shuffling feet draws nearer. She lifts her head to find a grinning boy standing shoulder to shoulder with Baine. Not wanting to look the boy in the eye, she lowers her head slightly and is greeted by the skeletal face of an angry clown resting between the teeth of his jacket zipper. The zipper teeth widen as the boy extends his arms wide like a circus grandmaster, "Ladies and gentleman….," circus boy says as if he's talking to a large audience.

"It look like there some fucking ladies out here?" Baine interrupts, his freckles turning a fiery red.

Sunni drops her head. She secretly considers herself a lady on good days and despises the entire concept on others. But the idea of not being considered a lady at all feels humiliating. Circus boy chuckles, gives a goofy grin and pipes up a correction, "Faggots and gentleman!"

"You saying I hang with fags now?" Baine's freckles seem to grow into pulsating suns.

Circus boy's goofy grin disappears. "That ain't what I meant...," he says.

Sunni smirks at the conflict. For a moment it's as if she is just one of the guys participating in some twisted joke. But the feeling of normality doesn't last. Baine gives circus boy one last nasty look and then squats in front of Sunni. He is so close that Sunni smells the deep musty funk of his unwashed body. With each breath Sunni takes, her anxiety level rises. She nervously rubs the silver ring on her middle finger and avoids eye contact as the other boys close in on her from all sides.

Circus boy's voice lowers to a conspiratorial whisper, "Live and in person...."

Baine plucks a sardine tin from the snow and holds it up for examination. "Who am I?" he asks Sunni.

Circus boy chimes in without missing a beat, "Pimp 007!"

"Shut the fuck up!" Baine presses the edge of the sardine tin into Sunni's forehead forcing her to lift her gaze. "I want her to answer."

Sunni's brow furrows and her lips purse as Baine taps the sardine tin against her forehead...one...two...three times. Sunni's eyes shutter closed.

"Look at me!" Baines blares.

Sunni's eyes open again, narrowed and intense. "The collector," she says.

Baine smiles with satisfaction. He shifts the sardine can into her line of sight just as Circus boy steps closer.

"Give her some money," circus boy says and the other boys hum a collective agreement.

"I ain't giving her shit," Baine retorts. He reaches into his back pocket just as the streetlights flicker on. "She the one that should be paying...ain't that right?" He pulls out a switchblade and flicks it open like a seasoned pro. Sunni focuses on the blade and her breathing grows panicky. Her eyes shift to the boys as she frantically searches the crowd for a sympathetic face — she finds none. But wait, there is something. A glimmer in the eyes of one of the boys? Barely noticeable, Jin, a thin boy wearing a jacket two sizes too small is partially concealed in the crowd of boys. He wears a stiff smile but his eyes — is that sadness — regret? Jin notices Sunni watching him so he quickly averts his gaze focusing on the pink ballerina shoes instead.

But Jin isn't the only one who notices the exchange of glances. Baine locks onto Sunni's line of sight and his narrowed eyes settle on Jin, placing the boy in the spotlight. Baine's smile is a hybrid of a snarl and a grin as he speaks, "You got a fan."

Baine's declaration doesn't stop Sunni's staring. She continues to look, hoping to see those sympathetic eyes again; but Jin only lifts his gaze momentarily for fear of what it might reveal. Irked by the silent exchange of glances, Baine presses the cold blade into Sunni's neck — carefully. "He ain't the one you owing," he says.

Sunni lifts her chin and swallows hard as the cold steel presses against her skin. She can feel its sharp edge threatening to slice her neck wide open and she can sense that Baine's threat is no empty bluff. She wiggles her right leg; but keeps her gaze trained on Baine's intense eyes. "My shoe," she says, her voice just as shaky as her hands.

With a tilt of his head Baine orders circus boy to take off Sunni's shoe. The boy complies and discovers a fold of dollar bills and some change. He counts it. "Three dollars," circus boy says.

"That ain't enough." Baine removes the blade from Sunni's neck. "Take off your coat," he says as he slides the blade across her coat collar. Sunni's foot is already stinging from the winter cold; so she hesitates. Getting another coat would be tough. Her chipped fingernails lightly scratch at the zipper; but she's no closer to disrobing.

"Take it off her," Baine orders Jin.

Sunni watches Jin's face harden as he makes long, quick strides towards her. "I can do it," she says. She quickly unzips the down coat and hands it to Jin once he's standing before her. She peers up the length of the coat and into the boy's face catching another glimmer of regret; but the look quickly vanishes again as Jin takes the coat and steps to the side. Sunni lets her gaze linger on Jin's visage for a few moment's longer before lowering her gaze and folding her arms over her chest as she begins to shiver. Her flimsy pink and grey turtleneck is not enough to protect her from the winter chill. Her teeth begin to chatter as the boys continue to stand over her and Baine continues to watch. What else do they want, she asks herself; but she doesn't look up for fear that she might provoke them further. Baine tilts his head to the side and studies Sunni more intensely, a motion that makes Sunni's teeth chattering turn into a full out trembling of every part of her body.

Baine's enjoying every moment of her anxiety. He thrusts his fists towards her face as if he might hit the girl and she flinches as expected making Baine and the boys, except for Jin, laugh hard. Baine wipes his runny nose with the back of his hand, never taking his sights off of the trembling girl. "Put your arms down," he orders Sunni while pointing the tip of his knife at her.

But she doesn't move fast enough so he backhands her across the face sending her toppling onto her side. Another uproarious burst of laughter emits from the boys as Sunni's cheek hits a swirl of dirt and snow.

Her ear rings and her cheek stings as she plants her palms into the ground and tries to lift herself. But before she can right herself, Baine grabs her hair and smashes her face back into the dirty snow.

"Don't you ever fucking steal outta my city again, you fucking bitch!" Baine says as he straddles Sunni and bangs her head against the ground, his knife wielding hand only inches from her face. Sunni lets out a loud shriek and a dull throb lodges itself in her temple. Baine releases her hair and pulls the trembling girl up by the collar of her turtleneck. "Do you know what's gonna' happen to you if you steal out of my city again?" he asks while pointing his knife at her throat. Sunni wants to answer; but she can only respond with more tremors and a small gasp as she tries to find the word for yes.

"Huh?!" he demands. "I'm gonna show ya." He thrusts the blade forward and slashes it through the front of her turtleneck, splaying open the cottony fabric. The cold air sweeps across Sunni's chest and the boys hoot and holler as she lowers her gaze and tries to close the torn fabric.

"I said put your arms down," Baine says as he retracts his blade and shoves it back into his pocket. Sunni slowly lowers her hands and her head drops too. She tries hard to block out the boys' chuckles and snide remarks about her body. And she wishes herself invisible as she feels their gazes freely roaming over her chest. Her shoulders slump and her entire frame shrinks as the shame of her predicament weighs down on her.

"Lay down," Baine commands Sunni; but she freezes. "I said lay down!"

Sunni starts to lay face first in the snow; but Baine punches her in the back.

"On your back," he says. But Sunni doesn't comply. Convinced that they boys are going to hurt her no matter what, she decides she won't make it easy on them. Baine punches her again and tries to roll her onto her back; but she begins to flail her arms about, trying to grab, scratch and pound Baine's face; but her blows seem ineffectual. Baine is almost twice her size and works out regularly, so he's able to roll her over with one arm and with the other he snaps his fingers at Jin and says, "Hold her down." Jin moves one foot forward, but stops as Baine searches through his coat pockets even as Sunni continues to resist him.

"What ya' gonna do?" Jin asks.

"I said fucking hold her down!" Baine demands as he pulls a cell phone from his coat's inner pocket. But Jin doesn't move despite knowing the consequences.

To his relief, circus boy jumps in and grabs Sunni's flailing arms.

A southern man's voice booms from behind the crowd of boys,

"What you boys doing back here?"

The boys turn to find Police Captain Danaski sitting in his patrol car about ten feet away. The loud rattle of the car engine booms against the hush of silence that's fallen over the boys. Baine stands and motions for his fellow hunters to not move one inch. But upon seeing the Captain the boy holding Sunni releases her and she is able to roll onto her side and pull her turtleneck closed.

Baine manages a smirk. "Finally," he bellows out as the Captain steps out of the police cruiser with his baton at the ready. His tall, sturdy build belies the fact that he's a man well over 60 years old. The Captain shifts his eyes to Sunni as she struggles to her hands and knees, then he moves his focus to Baine. "What in the world you got going here, boy?" he asks.

Baine pipes up again. "Caught a thief Captain!" he says with all the indignation he can muster.

Clamping her torn turtleneck closed, Sunni rests on her shins. "It ain't true," she murmurs and once again looks to Jin as he slowly steps towards her. The movement catches Baine off guard as he counters Sunni's denial. "It's the truth. Ain't got no receipt for this," he says as he kicks the box of crackers. His eyes stretch open in shock as Jin hands Sunni her coat.

"Your daddy know you out here fucking with his property?" the Captain asks.

Baine peels his eyes off of Jin and his voice falters at the mention of his father, "It ain't like that at all, Captain."

The Captain waves him off. "Go on...getcha' self on home or wherever ya' headed," he says.

"But what about this stuff...," Baine says as he puffs up, trying hard to stay tough.

"Go on now, don't make me say it twice," the Captain says as he eyes all of the boys.

Baine takes another hateful look at Sunni; he's been warned to not make trouble with the Captain so he backs down. Pursing his lips he motions for his crew to move out. They follow him down the road while Jin takes off in the opposite direction.

The Captain moves closer to Sunni as she comes to her knees again and manages to zip her jacket. The weight of humiliation leaves her kneeling for an extended amount of time, her head bowed.

The Captain shoves the tip of his baton under her chin, forcing her to lift her head. But she refuses look at him.

"Getcha' things together, we going down to the station," he says, retracting his baton.

Hands trembling, Sunni slowly comes to her feet and picks up her things. She stuffs them into her satchel and stands hunched forward trembling from the cold, still not daring to look at the Captain.

"Get in the car," the Captain says coldly.

Much of the back roads have been returned to gravel and the main streets are marred with crater like potholes, so the trip to the station is bumpy, tossing Sunni up and down in the backseat of the patrol car. Sunni steals a glance of the Captain, painfully aware that his eyes are on her just as much as the road. "What was that about back there?" he asks in a flat, conversational tone, as if asking her about the weather. She stares out the window not answering, careful to note each street they pass and which way they turn. "Left on Jefferson, right on First, two blocks left by the Mariposa tree," she repeats silently to herself, arms folded tightly across her chest, she is grateful her zipper wasn't broken, grateful she managed to salvage a sliver of dignity.

"You really want to play this game?" The Captain presses further.

"No sir," Sunni responds weakly.

"Well?" he asks again.

Sunni lowers her head and clutches at the zipper of her jacket. The Captain glances at her, his gaze hard.

"You running some independent operation in my town, Sunni?"

"No!" she says forcefully, looking at him in the rearview mirror.

"Because if you are, you know imma' find out about it," he says sternly. "Ain't nothing a secret from me in this town."

Sunni jerks her gaze away and once again looks out the window. "Monroe, Washington, abandoned house on Washington, blue, check back door," she silently says to herself. Quiet falls over the patrol car for a few moments, only the local bums are heard squabbling as they drive past a small tent city, minus the tents.

"Them boys why I ain't seen you around?" the Captain finally asks.

Once again Sunni doesn't respond.

He turns to look at her. "I ain't spending enough quality time with ya'? Is that what it is?"

Sunni doesn't respond. They pull into the police station parking lot. "Let's fix that then," the Captain suggests as he parks the car. Sunni tries to even out her breathing as the Captain steps out of the cruiser and opens the back door. "Let's go," he says as he grabs Sunni's arm and pulls her out of the car. The parking lot is half full with old tattered police cruisers, many with broken taillights and dented fenders. Sunni stares into the shadowy places broken streetlamps are unable to illuminate and finds a stray cat curled under a police car that's still warm from a recent patrol.

She's shoved forward by the Captain and they make their way towards the entrance, both of them watchful as they tread over the ice that covers many parts of the lot.

***

Perched at his corner desk, Officer Tony Gavilan takes a long drag on his cigarette. His dark brown hair is short and scraggily, a perfect match for the scruffy stubble on his face. Tony's tired gaze lifts from the blackened ashtray and rests on Sunni as she enters the police station with the Captain. Their eyes meet, but only for a moment before Sunni quickly turns away and disappears inside the Captain's office. Tony blows out a long train of smoke letting his gaze linger on the closed door.

"Didn't take long for her to find trouble," Tony says as he shifts his attention to Officer Carlos Ramirez who stands on the other side of his desk nursing a lukewarm cup of coffee.

"It's a damn shame, isn't it?" Carlos asks as he sits the cup of coffee on Tony's desk.

Tony takes another hard drag on his cigarette, letting the smoke fill his lungs and relax his muscles. "Yeah, it is," he finally says as he blows out a plume of smoke and squashes the butt in the ashtray.

Carlos frowns and nods his head in eager agreement, "That's the problem with this town, apple don't fall far from the tree," he says and then continues on without taking a breath, "If the parents of these kids would just…." Carlos' voice suddenly trails off as he notices Tony become very still, his vacant gaze fixed on the surface of the worn down desk and his hand resting on the extinguished cigarette butt. The memory of his dead daughter pushes itself to the forefront of Tony's mind. He closes his eyes trying to shut out the thought; but he can't. He can only see the needle stuck in his daughter's arm and her dead eyes looking up at him. He twists his head slightly to the side and presses the cigarette butt deeper into the ashtray as he tries to think of something else, anything else besides his daughter's body filled with a deadly dose of meth. Carlos' frown melds into a mask of regret as he speaks to Tony in a much softer voice, "Look Tony, I didn't mean nothing by that…," he trails off again, not sure what to say. "What I meant to say," he starts again. "I meant…."

Tony raises his hand and shakes his head. "Don't sugarcoat it on account of me," he says. "The truth is that a weak parent makes a weak child. I know that better than anyone in this fucking station. So you don't need to sugarcoat it on account of me, all right?"

Tony peers into Carlos' face with his intense brown eyes, his thin lips strained into a snarl.

"All right," Carlos says.

Tony looks away. He's not mad at Carlos, not really, he's mad at himself and the world. He lights up another cigarette and takes a deep puff. "We're lucky to have a man like the Captain in this town," he says as he blows out another stream of smoke.

"Yeah, we are," Carlos says. "Look, Tony…I…"

Tony interrupts, his intense brown eyes on Carlos again, but his snarl gone, "How long we been friends, Carlos?"

Carlos shakes his head and chuckles nervously. "Too long," he says.

"Then you know you don't need to sugarcoat the truth on account of me, right?" Tony asks.

"Yeah, but—," Carlos starts to respond but is again interrupted.

"No buts," Tony says as he comes to his feet and slips his dingy police cap over his scraggily brown hair. "Truth is the truth," he continues. "No matter who it's about." He grabs his threadbare police jacket and slips his arms into it. Every other button is missing, but he manages to close it anyway. He gives Carlos a friendly pat on the shoulder and a determined smile. "Merry Christmas," he says, and heads towards the station's exit.

***

The Captain's office is more than just an office, it's a testament to the respect New Hope City has for the man. Framed photographs of him and the kids he has spent the past 15 years nurturing, adorn the walls. They stand alongside awards and accolades celebrating his willingness to work in a town that most had forgotten long before the final crash. The Captain stands behind his large mahogany desk talking on the phone as he zips up his trousers. His service belt and jacket lay across the desk next to a glass of ice water. Leaned against the wall nearest the door and clutching her satchel close to her chest, Sunni watches as the Captain slams his phone shut and trains his gaze on her.

"Why you acting like that?" the Captain asks as Sunni presses her satchel deeper into her chest, lowers her gaze and struggles with an overwhelming nauseous feeling. Staring at the cracked and dusty tile floor, Sunni shakes her head. "You promised that I didn't have to do this no more," she murmurs, her voice barely more than a whisper.

The Captain sighs. "Well ya' made a lot of promises you ain't kept either, so I guess that makes us about even," he says. He grabs the glass of ice water and takes a few gulps. Sitting the half empty glass back on the desk, he once again trains his gaze on the girl. "Wash it down with this," he says pushing the glass towards the edge of the desk.

Sunni takes a few reticent steps towards the desk; but she doesn't reach for the glass of water.

"Go on now," the Captain says.

Sunni takes a few more steps forward and grabs the glass, forcing the water down her throat and nearly vomiting it all up; but she doesn't dare. She swallows it all and rests the empty glass on the desk, right in ring of moisture left behind because she knows the Captain is particular about keeping order to things. She lets her gaze wander towards the Captain's face just to be sure and he gives her a reassuring nod.

"It true what Baine said about you stealing?" the Captain asks as he wraps his duty belt around his waist.

Sunni tenses, not wanting to lie; but not wanting to tell the truth either. But she doesn't need to; her silence is answer enough for the Captain. Besides, he figured she had been stealing.

"Where's the money I gave your mama?" the Captain asks, another question he already knows the answer to.

Averting her gaze again, Sunni quickly shakes her head and answers with a scratchy voice, "I don't know."

The Captain makes some final adjustments to his duty belt and digs his wallet out of his pocket. Plucking a twenty dollar bill from the worn black leather bill fold, he catches a glimpse of Sunni's surprised expression. "You know I always give a little something extra," he says as he slides the money across the desk and towards the girl who looks at it suspiciously.

"That means you gonna' owe me now," the Captain says confirming that the little something extra has strings attached. Sunni doesn't reach for the money. She lowers her gaze again and remains frozen in place.

The Captain frowns at the girl's silent refusal. "Sunni?... Go on now, take it...you owe me anyway."

Sunni slowly slides the twenty dollar bill off the desk and slips it into her sneaker.

Putting on his jacket, the Captain walks around the desk and towards the door.

Sunni finally speaks, "My mom coming?"

"We gonna' getcha' a ride home," the Captain says as he opens the door and steps into the buzz of the station. He calls out, "Who off duty right about now?"

Carlos answers, "Gavilan just left, but you might can catch him."

"You do that now," the Captain orders Carlos and then motions for Sunni to follow him. They make their way towards the station's exit.

***

Sitting in the back of Tony's patrol car, Sunni stares out the window as they drive past the boarded up buildings and general squalor of downtown New Hope. She can feel Tony watching her in the rearview mirror. "Got yourself in a bit of trouble?" he asks.

Sunni fingers the strap of her satchel and peels her gaze from the window to look at Tony. "Uh...," she mumbles, not knowing how to answer that question— it seems that trouble finds her.

Tony adjusts the rearview mirror and says, "I haven't seen you around here too much. Just got here a few months back, right?"

Sunni nods. "Yes...."

"How you finding it so far?" he asks.

Sunni lowers her gaze and decides it's best to not answer truthfully. "Fine," she says.

"Captain getting you use to how things go around here?" Tony glances over his shoulder to get a better look at the girl.

Sunni doesn't look at him, she only nods and offers a "Mmmhmm."

Tony returns his gaze to the road and takes a left into the trailer park entrance. He needs no directions; he knows exactly where the girl lives. He remembers when she first moved in. He pulls up to a battered looking trailer and parks the police cruiser. Before Tony and Sunni can completely step out of the cruiser, Shannon is already standing in the doorway wearing a white housecoat and beige slippers. A small puppy barks at her heels and a cigarette dangles from her lips as she hastily makes her way down the steps and towards Sunni.

Sunni can smell the choking stream of smoke as she closes the car door, "Mom—" An open handed slap lands on the bridge of Sunni's nose stopping her midsentence. The girl shields her face with her arms; but it's only partly effective against her mother's wild blows.

"Shut up! Shut the fuck up! This the shit I'm tired of!" Shannon tries to pry Sunni's arms away from her face; but her grip is broken when Tony steps between them and twists Shannon's arms behind her back.

"Ma'am!" Tony says as he tightens his grip and Shannon struggles to wrench herself free. "I need you to calm down!" This isn't really his beat and he can already feel himself taking his frustrations out on the woman.

The puppy growls and barks at Tony's feet as the conflict escalates.

"I didn't do nothing!" Sunni backs away until she is pressed against the police cruiser. She checks her nose for blood and anxiously watches Tony wrangle her mother. She doesn't want trouble. She figures the worse he makes it for her mom, the worse her mom will make it for her. "It's okay...don't...," she begins to plead with Tony.

Tony glances at the rattled girl. He starts to yell at her; but he doesn't. He can sense the fear and decides it's best to avoid the paperwork of taking the woman down to the station. "You going to stay calm?" he asks Shannon. She scowls but gives a nod of agreement. Satisfied with her response, Tony slowly releases her.

Shannon massages her arms and glares at Sunni. "Get in the house!" She points towards the trailer door. Sunni quickly pushes off the cruiser and moves towards the trailer door as Tony pulls out a pack of cigarettes and lights another smoke. She can feel Tony's eyes on her again as she steps into the trailer with her mother and the whining puppy right behind her.

Sunni is startled as her mother slams the trailer door closed. With trembling hands, she gently sits her satchel on the floor by the door and squints to see her mother's face in the mostly dark trailer. Only a splatter of light from a neighbor's outdoor Christmas lighting trickles through the window and washes over her mother's face.

Shannon pulls the cigarette from her lips and expels a plume of smoke. "You know not to start no trouble with the Captain," she says.

"I wasn't doing nothing…," Sunni says and glances out the window as the police cruiser's engine revs up and Tony drives away. She turns towards her mother again as the woman returns the cigarette to her lips and grabs a heavy duty trash bag.

"That ain't what the Captain say," Shannon says as she hastily stuffs the trash bag with clothes, shoes, papers and other odds and ends. Sunni studies every object.

"Just was doing what you told me to," Sunni mumbles.

Shannon pauses her gathering of various objects and narrows her eyes at Sunni. "Working?" She blows out another plume of smoke. "Cause if you been working I want my cut."

Sunni casts her gaze downward, watching the puppy roll around scratching his back on the green carpet. For a moment she considers the twenty dollars in her shoe but decides against mentioning it.

"Useless," Shannon hisses as she continues to stuff things into her bag.

Sure that her mother's angry gaze is no longer there to greet her, Sunni looks up again. She watches her mother scurry around the messy room, picking over piles of clothes and mounds of paper before choosing this or that to stuff into her bag. She takes a few tentative steps towards her mother. "Going on another trip?" Sunni asks.

Shannon stops her collection of objects; but she doesn't look at Sunni. Instead, she gives her the instructions she has been rehearsing all evening. "Every Sunday St. Thaddeus Parish got dinner at 3 o'clock, it really don't get started until five; but you best be there by three in line, Sunni." She sits the trash bag on the table. "They can get real huffy if ya' eating but ain't attending their services, so…" she trails off and finally forces herself to look at her daughter. She glances over Sunni's soiled clothing and frowns. "Wear your church clothes."

Their gazes meet and for a moment there is a connection.

Or at least Sunni thinks there is a connection. Well, if there is a connection, it would be a first — the first in a long time. Sunni lowers her head and focuses on the folded edge of the heavy duty trash bag before she silently walks past her mother and into the kitchen. "You going to be gone long this time?" she asks as she opens the fridge and finds it empty except for a stale slice of her favorite cake which she enjoys baking when she can find the ingredients. Getting no answer from her mom, she slowly closes the fridge door and turns to face her mom again.

"Can I come with you this time?" she asks as she leans her back against the fridge.

Shannon resumes the shoving of objects into the trash bag. "Come with me for what, Sunni?" There's a hard edge to her voice.

Sunni shrugs and finds herself at a loss for words; but finally says, "I was just hoping that this time...."

Shannon sits her bag on the table and makes her way towards the kitchen. Face-to-face with her daughter, her expression softens as she sighs out another stream of smoke. "Ain't no this time, Sunni."

Sunni furrows her brow in confusion. "But you said—"

Shannon cuts her off and continues, "What I said is that...that you getting old enough now...." She pulls the cigarette from her lips again and frowns at the slight pang of guilt and pity needling her. She shakes her head, hoping to shake off that feeling. For a moment she considers backpedaling on her decision; but she shakes that thought off too. Her mind is made up, things are what they are and this is it—the end. The thought of finality gives her a rush of relief which brings a smile to her face. "How you gonna' make it without me?" she asks with pride. A part of Shannon feels the need to be needed but another part, the majority part, feels stifled by it. She brushes a stray hair out of Sunni's face. A car horn blares. Shannon quickly retracts her hand. "You will make it, just like I did," she says, and walks back towards the living room.

Sunni hunches forward unable to move. It's as if someone has punched her in the gut. Moments pass before she finds the strength to push herself off the fridge and follow her mom into the living room. She doesn't bother to hide her fright as she grabs her mother's arm. "When you coming back?"

Shannon yanks away. "We been over this Sunni," she says curtly as she picks up the trash bag and swings it over her shoulder. The car horn blares again. The metallic taste of fear fills Sunni's mouth as her mother walks around her and heads towards the trailer's front door. Once again Sunni follows her, her eyes wide and glassy. She wraps her arms tight over her chest as they pause at the door. "Can I come with you? Please...," Sunni pleads.

"Don't do that," Shannon says as she opens the front door and looks back at her daughter. "I done gave you everything you need, that's all I got." Her voice rings with resentment, a resentment that stings Sunni. Shannon's gaze softens once more before turning her back on her daughter and stepping into the cold winter air. She quickly makes way down the steps. Sunni follows.

"Mom?" Sunni nearly trips over the puppy as he barks and whines at Shannon's heels. But Shannon's pace only quickens.

"Mom!" Sunni tries to block her mother's path; but Shannon doesn't even look at her, not even once — a fact that sends Sunni to the edge of a panic attack. "Mama!!" A few neighbors peek out of their windows as Shannon opens the car door. Sunni peers into the vehicle as if knowing the driver will somehow change things or give her some advantage.

"Get out of the way Sunni!" Shannon pulls the girl away from the car. She throws her trash bag into the backseat and hops into the front seat. And without looking at her daughter she slams the door closed. Sunni stands there silent, watching the Cadillac go into gear, back up a few inches and then rev forward and away from the curb. Blurry taillights grow distant in the flurry of snow. And after a few minutes Sunni stands alone on the empty street with her puppy whining at her feet.

Sunni's arms stiffen and her fingers tremble as she stands in the street looking down the empty road. She takes a big gulp of air and the chill scratches her lungs. Another gulp and another until she's unable to hold back the stream of sobs. Her puppy licks her sneakers and presses his paws against her shins just before her knees give way and she finds herself kneeling on the cold gravel road.

Did anyone see her mama leave? How is she going to eat? Who's going to look after her now? She combs her trembling fingers through her puppy's fur as she contemplates what just happened. It's getting cold, too cold to be kneeling in the street. She figures she should be careful less she get stuck that way. She forces herself to her feet and scoops her puppy into her arms. Looking down the road once more, she looks for any sign that her mother has had a change of heart; but she finds nothing; just more black emptiness. Her heart thumps a little harder as she presses her puppy's warm body against her own and makes her way back into the trailer.

Chapter 3

Sunni groans as she awakes, the puppy already gone to a warmer spot under the couch, a kitchen chair shoved under the front door handle, four empty cans of sardines on the floor and a butcher knife on the coffee table — only an arm's length away. She slowly pulls herself to a sitting position and touches the wet spot on her jeans. "Shit!" She studies the blood on her fingertips for a moment and then wipes it onto her pants leg. She can never keep up with her monthly visitor which isn't exactly monthly. With no calendar to speak of, the days often run together. Sunday is sometimes the same as Monday depending on where she's living or what she's doing. Two piles of dirty laundry lean against the wall, one for Sunni and the other for her mother. "Fucking slob," she cusses the laundry, as she rifles through her pile. She sniffs a pair of panties; not exactly clean but clean enough.

Sunlight bounces off the cracked vanity mirror as Sunni steps into the tiny bathroom. It's the only clean spot in the entire trailer. Mama is neurotic about a clean bathroom. Sunni peels off her blood soaked jeans and underwear and shivers as her bare feet press against the cold linoleum floor. She turns the sink's knob; but no water comes out. She lets out a huff. It's the second time this month the taps have run dry and it's not for lack of paying the bill. She bangs her hand against the wash basin and looks around as if water might spout from the walls. After a few moments of frustration her gaze falls on the toilet. She lifts the lid. There's water there and it looks pretty clean. Not exactly clean; but clean enough. She snatches a washcloth off the towel rack and grabs a sliver of soap. And just as she's dipping her washcloth into the toilet bowl water, her thoughts drift back to her mother. The thought of mom never coming back makes her heart pound. She never really liked the woman; but being without her is more terrifying than the days when she's gone on a hitting spree. That's what Sunni calls it when mom gets too angry and loses control of herself. She gives the damp washcloth a few rubs against the sliver of soap and carefully washes herself. Getting clean enough is important to Sunni, just as important as staying alive.

Okay, maybe not that important. But it is the thought of staying alive that pervades Sunni's thoughts as she flips her clean enough underwear inside out and slips them on.

Looking clean makes you look cared about. And people who are cared about don't get messed with as much. She jogs back into the living room and quickly finds a new pair of jeans. The puppy is still asleep under the couch; so she decides to not rouse him. She doesn't want him begging for food and water she doesn't have. As quietly as she can, Sunni slips on her jeans, shoes and coat. She tenuously ogles the butcher knife on the coffee table. Will she need it? Anything is possible in this town, she tells herself. She snatches up the knife and slips it into her inner coat pocket. The sudden motion jogs the puppy out of his slumber. For a few moments he watches Sunni as she zips up her coat, then he scampers across the room just as she is unhooking the kitchen chair from the trailer's front door.

"You can't come with me." Sunni squats and pets the puppy. It's just them now, the two of them against the world. It's a sad thought because the puppy wouldn't bite a fly even if its life depended on it.

The dog whines and begs for more attention. Sunni gives him a big hug and a little kiss. "You stay here, okay? I won't be long. I'll get ya' some treats. Your favorite," she promises. The money is tight, as always. But she figures she can find a little something special with her favorite ball of fur in the whole wide universe.

The puppy whines again; but Sunni ignores it. She grabs her satchel, throws it over her shoulder and turns towards the door. "Never like it when you don't get your way now do you?" She proceeds to unlock the door — all four locks. She has a system. Top locks first but only when exiting the trailer. She opens the door and steps outside, sticking her foot out to force the puppy inside the trailer. "Stay! Keep guard!" She closes the door and locks it — all four locks. This time bottom locks first.

Chapter 4

New Hope looks just like every other shithole town Sunni has lived in over the past four years since the final great crash, but today it seems more depressing. She tries to shake the feeling that this time is different and convinces herself that her mom is just pulling her regular shit and that she'll be back soon enough, in the meantime she has to survive. As she passes a pair of burnt out buildings Sunni steps off the sidewalk and into the street, keeping a considerable distance between herself and the place where trouble lurks. She knows how to stay safe, most times. She continues on, her eyes cast downward. Two homeless men sit on plastic crates watching her. She keeps her head lowered. Show humility, even misery and they won't bother you, she tells herself. And she does just that, passing the men who only give a satisfied smirk. Misery is the type of currency that buys a girl like Sunni a temporary pass, a reprieve from violence and humiliation. If a person is already miserable why knock them down further, so goes the logic. But only the decent follow that logic and most aren't that decent in New Hope, at least not according to Sunni. The familiar, if not exactly elegant sign outside the local grocery interrupts Sunni's thoughts. She steps inside. She needs to get the essentials first. She shifts her right foot in her sneaker just to make sure her cash is still wedged in there. Raj, a balding man with a heavy foreign accent watches the girl suspiciously.

"What is it that you want?" he asks and only partly attempts to sound helpful as he leans over the counter. Sunni jumps at Raj's gruff voice. She reflexively looks at him but then quickly refocuses her attention on the badly stained concrete floor, "No...uhm..." She eases her gaze towards the feminine products aisle, "...nothing," she concludes as she makes her way to the adjacent aisle filled with chips, cookies, crackers and an assortment of canned foods.

She picks up a couple of cans of chicken noodle soup. As she makes her way further down the aisle, Raj decides to take no chances and quickly repositions himself at the entrance of the aisle making it known that he's watching her. Sunni glances over her shoulder for only a moment, she's use to it. She makes a sharp right and then another sharp right placing her in the aisle with the feminine products sandwiched between the condoms and adult diapers. She lingers by the adult diapers pretending to look at them.

"For your grandfather," Raj says as he peers at her from the adjacent aisle. His looming height and the short shelving of the shop allow him to peer over the top of the aisle at Sunni.

"Huh?" Sunni is surprised by his comment although she knows he's watching her.

Raj joins her in the aisle and grabs one of the adult diaper packages. "This super absorbent, better," he says as he hands it to her, truly trying to offer some assistance.

Sunni falls silent and blindly grabs a package of sanitary napkins. "He likes this one better." She avoids eye contact and quickly walks past Raj, making her way to the counter. Raj shoves the adult diapers back onto the shelf and shakes his head as he follows her. He watches Sunni dig money out of her shoe and finally gets a good look at the girl's face when she stands upright. Repositioning himself behind the counter, it dawns on Raj, "You don't have a grandfather!"—he points at her—"You the thief!" Sunni's face grows hot as if it is the middle of August instead of just a few days before Christmas. She keeps her gaze averted as she impatiently waits for Raj to ring up her items. But he doesn't touch the cash register; instead he continues to berate her, calling her a thief and a disgrace. Her eyes remain focused on the sticker covered counter as she slowly unfolds the twenty dollar bill. She always tries to keep a low-profile, eyes averted, hood over her long black tresses, moving about town at odd hours, but once in a while her careful attempts at invisibility fail and she is noticed. Her hands tremble as she pushes the cash across the counter towards Raj. "I'm not...it wasn't me," she lies, her voice muffled. But Raj only snarls at her as he grabs the money and finally rings up the purchase. All the feral kids in New Hope look alike to him, so he's not 100 percent sure it is her. But she's as good a target as any. They are all guilty in his eyes. Instinctively he makes change, $2.30; but for a moment he considers keeping the money for himself. He considers it a debt owed to him. Against her better judgment Sunni looks him in the face, she needs that money and her expression lets him know it.

Raj lifts his fist, the balled up cash and change pressing against his palm. Another moment of hesitation and then he tosses all of it onto the floor. It lands a few inches away from Sunni's feet; but she doesn't dare kneel down to pick it up. It's the little bits of dignity that she is determined to hold on to.

Although she badly needs every penny, she grabs her things and walks by the change scattered across the stained concrete floor. She shoves her sanitary napkins and cans of noodle soup into her satchel and exits the store.

Head still bowed, Sunni quickly makes her way into the street; snow flurries once again begin to fall. Her hands clutching the strap of her satchel, she passes a boarded up bank, a shuttered café and a gutted shopping complex which threatens to topple over. A familiar voice stops her forward motion.

Her eyes roll up. It's Baine—and his crew, only a few feet away, engaged in what seems like a serious conversation. Her breathing stops, she starts to back up; but she's spotted. One of Baine's crew has his eyes fixed on her. Run? Her knees bend as she readies her body for flight. The butcher knife pressing against her chest reminds her that she's not totally helpless this time. She curses her own folly. How many of them could she take down before she's overcome and slashed with her own blade? Stupid, she curses herself again. Her eyes lock onto the boy staring at her and then it dawns on her—it's kind eyes, Jin. Jin lets his gaze linger for only a moment longer before returning his attention to the conversation. Sunni continues her retreat, walking in the opposite direction. Don't run. Don't draw attention to yourself, she tells herself as she rounds the corner and disappears into the bustle of the homeless camp. It's the long way home; but she won't chance the open road. A local merchant stirs red paste like gruel in her large cast iron vat. Her soiled toothy grins greets Sunni as she pasts her. "Five dollars," the beige toothed woman yells out. "Five dollars for a bowl." That's actually cheap. Damn cheap. The price of food is high and most can't afford the basics like a bag of beans and rice let alone readymade grub. But for those living in the homeless camp with no way to cook or store their food, the gruel may be the only meal they get for a day or more. Sunni shakes her head and turns away from the woman, trying to not make eye contact with anyone else as she walks past a crying baby huddled with two older siblings under a weather worn tent. Sunni can feel their empty eyes watching her. She looks better off than most, just by virtue of having a coat with no holes in it and shoes that aren't too worn down. She clutches her satchel tight as she passes a ménage of men arguing over some meager possession. She quickens her pace making sure to take the shortest route towards the main road that will lead to her trailer nearly two miles away.

***

The sun beams down on the gravel road as Sunni makes her way through the trailer park entrance. The sun is bright like a summer day; but she can feel the winter chill oozing through her sneakers and nipping at the soles of her feet. Her cheap coat doesn't do much to keep the cold out either, so she crosses her arms over her chest to add a bit of warm. She carefully treads over the slick surface of the trailer park's gravel road which is mostly covered in snow, slush, and ice. Only a few feet from the trailer door, Sunni stops and her eyes widen when she notices a man standing on the porch. "Mom inside?" she asks hopefully; but her hope diminishes when the man turns and she realizes that it's not one of her mother's boyfriends.

"I was hoping you could tell me that," the pot bellied man says as he makes his way across the lawn of ice and mud. Holding a square sheet of paper, he points it at her as he speaks, "And don't tell me she at work, got enough of hearing that bullshit."

"She had to make a quick run out of town; but she'll be back shortly," Sunni says. "Something I can help ya' with?"

The man twists his lips in annoyance. "She's already two months behind and that little deposit she gave me ain't the type that can be cashed at a bank."

"She switched banks and there's a big mix up with it, say she'll get that to ya' right away," Sunni fumbles for the right combination of lies.

Her answer makes the man laugh hard. "Got to learn to lie better than that," he warns her. "Well, tell your mama that I'll be coming by with the Sheriff if she ain't paid by the date on this here notice." He hands Sunni the square sheet of paper and she studies the notice. She's use to getting them, but mama had always been around to come up with some quick plan to pack them up and move fast — this time is different.

The man walks past Sunni and makes his way down the road. Sunni watches him for a moment and then lets out a huff as if she had been holding her breath the entire time. She gives the notice another glance and makes her way up the steps of the trailer. Quickly unlocking the trailer door her frown disappears as the happy puppy leaps from its hind legs pawing at her thighs and furiously wagging his tail. "Down! Down boy!" Sunni says, a muted stream of giggles flowing from her lips as she makes her way to the kitchen and sits her satchel on the table. No matter how crappy things get her little pup is always there to cheer her up and that thought lifts her spirits a little. She plucks the can of chicken noodle soup out of her satchel. "It's just you and me, Sasha," she says as she rifles through the drawers searching for a can opener.

The puppy follows her every inch of the way. Sunni giggles again. "Yep, got your favorite," she says as she stops her search for the can opener and peers down at the dog incredulously or as incredulously as she can without having another giggle fit. "Wonder how much I can get for ya' at the church flea market?" she says, but she would never sell her puppy.

The puppy's ears lift and his head tilts to the side. Sunni turns back towards the counter and pulls the butcher knife from her inner coat pocket. Holding the soup can steady on the counter she punctures a few holes in the lid. For a few brief moments Sunni continues to giggle and feel hopeful as she pours the chicken noodle soup into the doggie bowel;

but the creeping feeling of dread returns as she takes a seat on the couch and watches Sasha lap up the soup. She grabs the eviction notice and reads it again, this time very carefully. She can't understand all of the words; but she knows exactly what it means. She flips the notice over and grabs a pencil with a dozen tiny chew marks on it. She does her calculations. She's better at counting than she is at reading and from what she can see the numbers don't look good. "Shouldn't have left that change Sasha, Mama always said pride be the end of me."

Chapter 5

Right before dawn Sunni carefully makes her way down the trailer steps carrying a 13 inch television. She places the TV atop a mountain of clothing and pillows piled into a rusty shopping cart. Other electronics, including a broken laptop and a small radio are safely tucked into two corners of the shopping cart. She covers the heap of valuables with a tattered blanket doing her best to conceal her bounty. Pulling her satchel over her shoulder she pushes the shopping cart down the gravel road of the trailer park and onto the uneven pavement of the city's main street. The trailer park's visage of cracked windows and cinder block steps display a discordant mixture of barely standing shelters. But soon the uneven pavement and decrepit trailers are left behind and smooth sidewalks and immaculately kept houses replace them as Sunni makes her way towards the church flea market. She pushes past the pretty houses, not daring to look to her side and peer into the wide open windows. She doesn't dare look at what is not and cannot be her life. But she can feel their presence, she can feel the houses mocking her and her predicament; but she presses on regardless until she comes to the red brick church with the large white steeple. There is already a long line although the sun hasn't come up yet. She pushes her cart to the back of the line where a middle-aged woman wearing a wide brimmed wool hat offers a quick greeting. "Morning," she says.

Sunni tilts her head up just a little to greet her. "Morning miss," she says, but then quickly averts her gaze as the middle-aged woman gives a satisfied grunt and returns to her gossipy chatter with the other ladies in line. Sunni burrows her pointy chin into her chest and blocks out the hum of their chatter. She half suspects that if she wasn't right behind them, she would be the next victim of their sharp tongues. Tightening her grip on her cart's handle and cutting her eyes to the right she watches a toddler snoozing comfortably in a stroller, a thick quilt covering everything but the child's shuttered eyelids.

She once again mentally calculates how much she can make off the stuff from her trailer. It's just enough to pay the rent; but not much more. Her chest tightens. What if mom comes back and gets mad because she's selling the last of their belongings?

She squeezes her eyes shut. Better than letting the Sherriff have it after she's thrown out onto the street. The line moves forward faster than she had hoped and after only thirty minutes she finds herself standing at the flea market entrance.

A stout woman with a round middle offers Sunni a stiff, overly friendly smile. "That'll be $25 little missy," she says as she stuffs a wad of five dollar bills into her fanny pouch.

Sunni shifts her foot in her sneaker, there isn't enough there. "Uhm...," she says, searching for the right response as she glances at the people waiting impatiently behind her. "Uhm right...I can get that to ya' after I...right when I'm leaving."

The stout woman's grin grows stiffer; but her voice is sickly sweet. "$25 for getting in and if ya' keep the place right, ya' get $20 of that back little Missy."

Sunni sighs anxiously and digs into her shoe. She pulls out a sweaty ten dollar bill and thrusts it towards the stout woman. "That's all I got. But I think I can make about $1000 on what I'm selling," she says. The moist ten dollar bill dissolves the stout woman's sugary smile and most of her manners. "I'm sorry little missy," she points to the sign which reads *$25 fee entrance $20 refundable, No exceptions*, "but it's the rules." Sunni again glances over her shoulder at the vendors behind her, many of them loudly displaying their annoyance. Sunni's gaze drifts back to the stout woman and she tries again, "But—" She is immediately cut off. "No buts little Missy," the stout woman says and then gives her attention to the next person in line. "Welcome to St. Jude Thaddeus," the stout woman says as she pastes on her plastic smile and takes the next patron's money. Sunni sighs and looks over the expanse towards the parking lot. She eyes the early birds setting up their tables. She hadn't sold at the market before so she never considered it would cost anything. Charging poor folks to sell their stuff didn't seem right at all to Sunni. She yanks her cart back from the entrance and begins to roll it across the narrow driveway and towards the church lawn. The size of a half football field, the winter brown foliage is more like a large bleak desert than a lawn.

"Little missy!" the stout woman yells out as Sunni rams her cart onto the church lawn. But Sunni doesn't stop. She pushes her shopping cart across the church lawn, completely ignoring the stay off the lawn sign.

"You can't do that!" the stout woman yells out. In the twenty-five years of St. Jude Thaddeus' existence no one has ever tried to get into the monthly swap meet without paying.

Sunni continues to push her cart across the grand lawn. If only she could get in and sell her stuff, she can pay the rent and have a place to stay — at least for now, she tells herself. She figures she can get at least $40 for the broken laptop before she even sets up her spot. She is halfway across the grand brown lawn when her cart's wheels begin to sink into the mud. But the quicksand like sinking of her cart doesn't deter Sunni; she just puts in even more pushing and shoving to get her cart and herself into the parking lot. Sirens blare, someone has called the cops. Sunni freezes in her tracks. She doesn't want another run in with the Captain. She turns to look over her shoulder. At this distance she can only see the blur of a cop jumping out of the cruiser but it's enough to send her into a panic. She takes off running, leaving her cart of goods behind. Sunni runs through the parking lot knocking over tables and people with the cop in hot pursuit. She hasn't even looked behind for fear of losing momentum. She jumps over a brick wall, dropping to her knees when she lands on the other side; but she quickly recovers. She starts to run again, but she discovers that it's a dead end. She spins around in search of another exit, only to find the cop struggling to climb over the brick wall. She finally gets a good look at him — it's Officer Tony Gavilan. Tony isn't out of shape, but he's no match for Sunni's agility, speed and youth. He grunts as he swings one leg, then another, over the top of the wall. Sunni backs up and looks around again. "Fuck!" she curses. And as soon as Tony's feet hit the ground he lunges towards the girl, slamming her into a metal dumpster and smashing her onto the ground. And before she can recover, Tony quickly rolls her onto her stomach and presses his knee into her back as she writhes and cusses.

"Calm down! I don't want to hurt you!" Tony yells as he pins her arms behind her back and yanks the handcuffs from his service belt.

"I didn't do anything," Sunni yells as the cold cuffs clamp around her wrists.

"Just calm down…I said I don't want to hurt you," Tony says as he presses her chest against the concrete and tightens the cuffs. Sunni groans as the dull edge of the handcuffs dig into her wrists and the chill of the concrete cuts through her coat. Tony rolls her onto her side. "I'm going to let you up, but you can't run," he says. "Is that understood?" Sunni's lips purse and her forehead wrinkles as she forces out a flustered "Yeah."

Tony grabs the girl's coat collar and tightens it around his fist. "This is my only warning," he says and then he pulls her to her feet. Sunni starts to pull away but the intense look in Tony's eyes stops her.

"Why did you run?" Tony demands, still slightly winded. A part of him resents being made to run around for something he views as trivial. A little trespassing is nothing in a town like New Hope. But when Sunni swallows nervously and fails to answer his question, Tony begins to suspect that the situation may be a lot more serious. He remembers her from the day before and frowns wondering what type of trouble she's creating now. "You steal that stuff back there?!" he asks.

Snapped out of her flustered silence, Sunni's eyes widen with indignation. "That's mine!" It's a golden rule of Sunni's, only steal when there are no other options and then it's not stealing at all. This way she sees herself not as a thief but something of a modern day Robin Hood. Steal from the rich and give to herself.

Tony relaxes his grasp on her coat collar. Most liars offer lengthy explanations, but her quick and brief response makes him lean towards believing her version of the story — so far so good. "All right, so tell me what happened then?"

Sunni once again grows flustered and a tired sigh escapes her lips as she begins to explain, "I just wanted to sell my stuff. I told her I could pay $10 now and another $15 later…." She tries to catch her breath as she's talking extremely fast. "I came a long way…and…." She stops, feeling angrier now as she fidgets her hands trying to find some way to get comfortable with the tight cuffs around her wrists. A wave of tears well up in her eyes. "I didn't do nothing wrong," she says. "Can ya' just please…can I just get my stuff and go? I promise…I won't come back."

The corners of Tony's mouth droop downward and his brows knit together as he studies the girl's teary but angry gaze. He releases her coat collar and grabs her by the arm. "Let's go," he says as he begins to lead her out of the alleyway. But Sunni leans away, only taking one step for his every two. "Am I going to jail?" she asks, her anger giving way to fear. Tony tightens his grip on her arm. "I told you, you getting only one warning," he says, and it's enough to get Sunni moving towards the exit of the alleyway.

The trek across the church grounds seems longer, colder and somehow more arduous than ever. Sunni can feel at least three dozen pairs of judgmental eyes on her back as Tony marches her to the entrance of the church flea market. Her hands securely cuffed behind her back, Sunni regrets that she can't at least put on her hood. No invisibility today. She can hear the stout gatekeeper's chatter cease as she and Tony come within just a few feet.

"Let me know what happened here?" Tony asks the stout woman who greets him with a scowl.

"I'll tell you what happened," she responds as she crosses her arms over her large breasts. "She didn't follow the rules…that's what happened," the stout woman huffs as she shifts her glare from Sunni to Tony. "She just think she's above it all, they all do—"

Tony cuts her off not bothering to hide his annoyance, "Do you want to file charges ma'am?" Sunni jerks her head up and stares wide-eyed at the cop. She doesn't want to go to jail. She doesn't want trouble from the Captain. She's about to pipe up a protest when the stout woman shakes her head. "No…no need for that…just need to get that mother of hers on board with raising her right." The stout woman nods her head to emphasize the point. "I tried to get her to go to service; but half the time she doesn't stay…," she continues her lecture as Tony's attention drifts. Tony cuts her off again. "Yeah…well, we'll get going then," he says as he adjusts his grip on Sunni's arm and guides her towards his police cruiser.

***

The shopping cart wheels protrude from the trunk of the police cruiser as the vehicle comes to a stop in front of Sunni's trailer. Tony steps out quickly, opening the back door for Sunni. He uncuffs her; but he doesn't bother unknotting the thin rope which keeps Sunni's things inside the trunk, he just slices it free with a utility knife.

"Got help to bring this stuff in the house?" he asks the girl.

Sunni shakes her head as she steps out of the cruiser and walks briskly towards the tail end of it. Her slender, petite legs come to an abrupt stop at the open trunk and she grabs the lightest thing she can carry — an old faux antique lamp for which she had created the most perfect sales lie. She sighs at the lost cash she's sure the lamp could bring her. As Tony lugs the 13 inch television up the steps of the trailer, she lingers by the trunk watching him. She's failed to get the rent, so right about now might be the time to make a run for it; but before she can make up her mind Tony casts a questioning glance in her direction. She hesitates, lowers her head, adjusts her fingers around the neck of the lamp and trudges up the stairs. As soon as she opens the trailer door, the blast of cold, putrid air bites at Tony's nostrils and the barking dog greets him. Tony kicks his way through debris which litters the floor as Sunni wrangles the pup. And after pushing aside a mess of dirty dishes he sits the TV on the small kitchen table. Glancing around the trailer for as far as his line of sight allows he takes it all in with a frown. Lowering his head for a moment he stares at a lone cockroach scurrying across the matted green carpet. Again he lifts his gaze and scrutinizes Sunni more carefully as she locks the puppy in the bathroom with a bowl of what looks like noodle soup and water.

"Where's your mom?" he asks.

"At work," Sunni answers quickly as she turns towards Tony and defensively folds her arms tightly across her chest.

Tony notices the posture. Right out of body language 101, the girl's got something to hide. "I know that's a lie," he says, taking on a defensive posture of his own. "How long she been gone this time?" He doesn't know Sunni or her mom personally; but he knows her story —it's typical. Negligent parent, troubled teen. Yada, yada, yada, same 'ole, same 'ole.

"She went to work this morning," Sunni says as she looks about the trailer, trying to rest her gaze on anything but the police officer.

Tony's eyes shift quickly giving Sunni a cutting look. "How many days this time?" His voice remains calm but his gaze intensifies. Sunni squirms under the scrutiny and struggles to find an answer or at least a good lie. Unfortunately she comes up with nothing. Tony leans against the kitchen table and sighs in disappointment. His worse suspicions confirmed. He figures the signs were evident when he first saw the woman move in with her daughter. Their things in trash bags, her skin gaunt and pale, her movements anxious and shaky, and then there was the procession of different men in and out of the trailer. He had a feeling she was an addict of some sort. But then again, there are so many addicts in New Hope. He steps past Sunni and out the trailer, making his way back to the trunk of his cruiser. He grabs the other items from the trunk and brings them into the trailer. Back and forth he goes, passing Sunni and saying nothing as she bites her nails and watches him. As he passes her a final time, he says, "Pack your things up."

Sunni stops biting her nails and watches him sit her other belongings on the living room floor; but she doesn't move to pack up anything. Tony adjusts his service belt and frowns. Here we go again. He feels like it's the same lecture, over and over. Each week, never changing. "You can't just stay here like this," he says as he motions to the filth in the trailer. "When your mom comes back—"

Sunni cuts him off, "If I'm not here, she won't know where—"

Tony raises his hand to stop her, his gaze falls on the square sheet of paper lying on the kitchen table. He reads it and then looks at her again, more questioning than annoyance.

"Your mom know you being evicted?"

"I ain't getting evicted."

"You're not exactly a good liar."

"She'll be back in time."

"Now you know you can't stay in this trailer by yourself."

"So what I'm supposed to do?"

"You can stay up by way of—"

"I ain't' going into fostering!"

"It's not like how you seeing it—"

"That's what they always say; but it's always worse...always worse than at home."

Sunni glances at the open trailer door; she could make a run for it.

"We don't have a choice," Tony insists. Sunni's gaze stays on the trailer door. Yes, she should make a run for it; but where would she go? She lets her gaze fall to the floor as she listens to her puppy's whines coming from the bathroom. No, running isn't the best option, not right now. She crosses her arms over her chest and swallows hard. She may need to barter with him; but is he the type? She forces herself to look up at Tony; but she's unable to look past his collar. It's always so hard to look them in the face. With an uncontrollable pounding in her chest she tightens her arms and finally speaks up, "Just tell me what I got to do." Sunni takes two steps forward so that she's only inches away from Tony. She unwraps her arms and presses her palms together in a prayer like form. Tony steels himself, stiffening his shoulders and legs as if the tiniest amount of desperate pleading could knock him over. Sunni forces herself to look him in the face and she searches his eyes for any sign of hope, any sign that he would show some pity, but she finds only cold resolution. Her gaze falls back to the green carpet and her voice shrinks, "Maybe we can…," her voice drops even further making it impossible for Tony to understand her.

"Speak up, girl!" he demands, becoming more impatient. There are a lot more problems out there that need solving and this girl is wasting his time.

Sunni drops her hands and finds the latch of her coat zipper. She pulls it open, but will he understand what she's offering?

"I said pack your things up!" he barks roughly, half tempted to yank her coat closed himself.

His harsh reprisal gives Sunni a terrible sense of fright; but she doesn't obey. She needs to make him understand that she has no intention of going into fostering, and that she's willing to pay any price to make sure of that. At least there is a price — all men have the same price. "You going to let me go, if…." She bows her head and her hair covers her face. Sometimes — times like this, the shame is too much to face.

Tony's impatience mixes with bewilderment as Sunni's hands drift down the length of her coat and rest at the waistband of her jeans. "What are you talking about?" he asks, but his eyes widen as Sunni fumbles to unbutton her pants. And as the girl tugs down her jeans, exposing the jut of her pelvic bone, Tony's wide-eyed gaze quickly shifts from Sunni's waistband to the cascade of black hair covering her face. What does she think this is?

Who does she think he is? "Pull your goddamn pants up, right now!" he says and he grabs her arm and yanks her out the door, to hell with her things; he'll let someone else handle that problem.

***

When the police cruiser stops in the driveway of the modest brick house, Sunni sits at attention, her palms pressed against the vinyl backseat and her grayish blue eyes peer through the partially fogged window. "I'm staying here?" she asks as Tony throws the gear into park and twists his torso to look at her. "Maybe, if you can keep you fucking pants on," Tony says. Forward facing again, he shoves the door open and bustles against the frigid wind. Taking a few short steps to the backdoor he hooks his gloved hand onto the handle and jerks the door ajar sending a flurry of snowflakes across Sunni's cheeks.

"Mrs. Danaski said it would be okay for you to stay with her for the night. Just as long as you understand the rules and don't cause no trouble," Tony says.

Sunni plants her feet on the compacted snow. Tony directs her towards the porch. "You know Mrs. Danaski?" he asks as they trudge across the snow and towards the crumbling concrete steps.

"Not really...," Sunni says, her response is snail's pace slow and slightly unsure with highlights of anxiety. "I mean...well... I know of her..."

Tony snorts at her response, he really doesn't give a damn if she knows the woman or not, he just wants to get rid of her at this point. They make their way up the crumbling concrete steps.

"You going back to get Sasha?" Sunni asks.

Tony gives a little frown, assuming she means the dog. "That's up to Mrs. Danaski," he says as he knocks hard on the steel door. Doorbells are overrated, plus it's a pure guessing game trying to figure out who's got electricity and on which days. Someone peers out the front window, a few moments pass before a petite woman in her mid-fifties appears in the doorway.

"Evening Mrs. Danaski,"—Tony removes his cap—"Sorry to come by so—"

"This her?" The woman's eyes widen in surprise at the sight of Sunni.

"Yes ma'am," Tony says.

Mrs. Danaski opens the door, her nightgown rustling in the cold night air. "Come here," she says to Sunni.

Sunni takes a few steps forward.

"Closer."

Sunni obeys and is eventually standing only a few inches away from the woman. Mrs. Danaski studies the girl, her face, her hair, her clothes. Sunni squirms under the woman's careful examination.

"Don't forget your manners," Tony glowers at Sunni.

"Evening...," Sunni says; but before she can continue Mrs. Danaski presses her index finger against the girl's lips.

"Not in my house," Mrs. Danaski says. She takes in Tony's perplexed expression. "Not in my house," she repeats firmly before stepping back into the house and slamming the door shut. Sunni stares at the door for a long stretch before lowering her head to study her sneakers.

Tony massages the bridge of his nose. "What just happened?" he asks. He finally looks at Sunni who is still studying her sneakers. "I thought you said you didn't know her."

"I don't…"

"When are going to stop lying?!" Tony shoves his cap back on his head. "Goddamn it! Let's go!"

They make their way back down the crumbling stairs. This is a problem, a big problem. New Hope's fostering system is just a collection of generous and sometimes selfish individuals willing to take in kids. Teens are always the hardest to place. Tony had high hopes that Ms. Danaski would be willing to take Sunni. Now he's out of options. They make their way down the walkway and get into the cruiser. Mrs. Danaski watches them from the window.

***

The drive back to the trailer park is punctuated with long, awkward silence. Sunni nervously squeezes her bottom lip between her index finger and her thumb as Tony parks the car in front of an unfamiliar trailer. Tony stares into the darkness for a long time, not moving, saying nothing and then he slowly turns to look at Sunni in the backseat. Her wide eyes stare back at him. He takes a look at his watch and lets out a small frustrated huff. "I've got patrol tonight," he says. He's half tempted to let her go; but if something happens to her it will be his problem. No, that's not true; it wouldn't be a problem for his job, only trouble for his conscious. Damn his conscious. He opens the driver's side door and steps out of the vehicle. Quickly pulling the back door ajar he blocks Sunni's exit. "You can stay here tonight," he says. His hand goes to his service belt. He doesn't fully trust her. And he knows he's asking for trouble; but he figures just this one time. But that's what he always says. "Put your hands behind your back." He unhooks his handcuffs. Sunni's eyes widen. "What? What for? I didn't run just like ya' told me," she says as she inches away from him, her eyes on the cuffs.

She tries to open the other door; but it won't budge. She gives it a frustrated punch. "Fuck!" she growls.

Tony leans into the car. "What's it going to be? Cause I can take you down to the station and let you spend the night in a cell until your mom gets back—from work," he says with a bit of sarcasm. Sunni presses her back against the locked door and scowls. She knows that he knows that her mom's not at work. And sitting down at the station for even a day is a lot worse than even the shittiest foster home.

"Fine!" she says as she extends her arms; wrists jammed together. "Just fucking do it!" Tony narrows his eyes. "You watch your filthy mouth with me," he says. He grabs Sunni's wrists and cuffs her. She doesn't say anything else as she is yanked out the car and led up the stairs of the trailer. Nicer than most of the boxy trailers in New Hope, the faded blue mobile home still begs for a fresh coat of paint and a new roof. They step inside. Sunni anxiously takes in the shabby but neat interior. Her troubled gaze falls on Tony as he pushes her towards the kitchen table. "Can I just stay at my own place…," she asks.

"Shut up," Tony says as he pushes down on her shoulder. "Kneel down." He motions towards the spot underneath the table. Sunni looks underneath the table but she doesn't kneel. "What you gonna' do?" she asks. His patience running even thinner, Tony purses his lips. "Just get under the table," he says. "This is for your own good." Sunni doesn't want to kneel under the table; but she does anyway because she doesn't see any other option. Tony quickly unsheathes a secondary pair of cuffs and locks her to the table base. "I won't be gone long," he says as he exits the trailer and heads to work.

***

Tony and Carlos patrol the streets of downtown New Hope, shining the cruiser's spotlight anytime they see something suspicious. "You got a shit detail with that kid today Tony," Carlos says. "Did you place her?"

Tony spins the steering wheel left and slowly takes the cruiser down a dark street. "Not yet."

Carlos looks surprised. "Not yet?"

"Nope."

Carlos' confusion and surprise remains plastered on his face. "Soooo….where is she?" The words drawn out by his southern drawl. Tony purses his lips and stalls by glancing down an alleyway.

"Tony…." Carlos sighs. "Here we go again."

"I've secured the prisoner," Tony retorts.

"At your house?"

Tony doesn't respond.

"At your house, Tony? How many times…shit it's like you looking for trouble, man."

Tony peers down another alleyway. He stops the car when he notices something. "Just trying to do my job….make a fucking difference, not like the rest of these cocksuckers." It is partly true, he wants to make a difference; but he's growing tired and while he won't admit it, also disillusioned with the process. He spins the steering wheel to the left and turns into a partially illuminated alleyway.

"You can't save everybody," Carlos lectures.

"I'm not trying to, just some."

Two figures scurry across the white beam of the police cruiser's headlights. Tony flicks on the siren and flashers and slams on the breaks. He and his partner hop out of the cruiser and pursue the suspects on foot. Tony's slim but muscular body is fast as he chases one of the figures. No longer hearing his partner's telltale thump, he assumes Carlos has gone after the other suspect. There's officially a curfew in New Hope and while most officers can't be bothered with trying to enforce it, Tony takes great care to enforce the letter of the law despite the tediousness of the task in a city flooded with crime. Tony finally catches up with the suspect and shoves him hard to the ground. As he struggles to cuff him, he begins to rattle off the guy's Miranda rights. The cuffs tight and snug, he rolls the suspect onto his back so he can see his face. "You!" Tony exclaims as he peers into Baine's freckled face.

"What you fucking with me for, I wasn't doing nothing," Baine growls. Tony gives the teen another hard shove onto the ground as he begins to pat him down.

"You got anything in your pockets that can cut or poke me?" Tony demands, sweeping his hands across Baine's torso and waist.

"Yeah, my fucking dick!"

Tony carefully searches Baines' pants pockets finding a cell phone and a small bag of crystal meth. He dangles the bag before Baine's eyes. "Don't look like your dick to me." Carlos jogs back to the alleyway out of breath and hunched over. "He got away," Carlos says, wiping the sweat from his face as Tony pulls Baine to his feet and marches him towards the cruiser. "You get a look at which way he went?" Tony asks.

Carlos shakes his head quickly as he catches a glimpse of Baine's hateful glare. "No, he just disappeared," he says as he hops into the cruiser and Tony shoves Baine into the backseat. Tony keeps the flashers and sirens going as he pulls out of the alleyway and heads back to the station.

***

Fatigue bubbling to the surface, Tony drags himself from the police station's lobby down a long, narrow hallway. A garish melody arrests Tony's stride. He plucks Baine's phone from the evidence bag and eyes the profile of the caller. A hard-edged scowl etches itself onto his lips when he sees the nude photo of a teenage girl. He quickly declines the call out of embarrassment more than anything else. Pausing in the hallway with a feeling of disgust, Tony tries to wipe the image from his mind. He hates it when the local kiddie hookers try to bribe him with their goods. 'A discount for you papa,' always makes him feel like a dirty old man. He glances over his shoulder towards the lobby to make sure no one else is nearby. The coast is clear. He begins to scroll through the contacts on Baine's phone. There may be something there he could use and he doesn't trust most of the staff to find it, let alone do anything with it if there is. A matter of fact, he half suspects that both the meth and the phone will mysteriously disappear once he checks them in. He chuckles as he realizes most of the names in Baine's contacts are girls, he never imagined Baine as a lady's man. He always seemed more like a loser in his mind. He scans over the names and thumbnail photos of various girls, including Sunni. And then he sees the name Lauren.

A terrible, nauseating feeling nearly overwhelms him. Certainly there had to be other Laurens in New Hope; but if that's the case Tony never met one. He seems to have trouble breathing. He swallows and massages his neck trying to rid himself of the choking feeling. He presses his index finger against the name opening the contact and revealing blonde hair, blue eyes, smiling face atop bare breasts. It is Lauren. All swagger and machismo vanishes. Tony's face crumples into a mask of despair. He quickly turns off the phone and ducks into the men's restroom. He rubs his hands across his face and hair and stands, unmoving, in the middle of the restroom. His mind filled with a jumble of thoughts, all of which are interrupted when the restroom door opens.

"Oh I didn't know you were in here," Carlos says as he moves towards one of the urinals. He eyes the bag of evidence in Tony's hand. "Checking that in?"

"Yeah of course," the words barely tumble out of Tony's mouth.

"You okay?"

Tony hesitates, still stunned and frozen. "Baine in the holding room?" he asks.

"Yeah, but you don't have to stay...I can handle it...."

But Tony has already left the restroom and is well on his way to the holding room before Carlos can finish his thoughts.

***

Lips fixed into a snarl, Tony examines Baine through the holding cell's plexiglass window. His right hand cuffed to a bar on the wall, Baine notices the man staring at him. "What the fuck you looking at? Go get me my fucking call?" he demands of Tony.

Tony steps into the holding cell, careful to keep his distance from the prisoner.

"Hey man, when I'm going to get my phone call?" Baine demands again.

Tony's gaze shifts to the window and out to the empty hallway. They're alone. He aims his gaze at Baine again and moves closer. "How did you know my daughter?"

At first Baine is shaken by the question, but then he shrouds his surprise with laughter and a dismissive air. "Man, everybody know your daughter."

Tony yanks his taser from his duty belt. "I'm going to ask you again? How did you know my daughter?"

Baine goes on the defensive, his apprehensive eyes scan the taser. "Don't you know who I am?"

Tony presses the taser against Baine's neck. "I know you won't be missed," Tony says in a monotone, trying hard to remain calm. "So let's try again, how did my daughter's picture get in your phone?"

"That's my private shit!" Baine says.

Tony jams the taser deeper into the flesh of Baine's neck and his cool façade quickly melts away. "What the fuck were you doing with my daughter's picture in your fucking phone?"

"Look man, I didn't have nothing to do with that girl dying!"

"What?" Now it's Tony's turn to be surprised. Baine's words challenge his understanding of things. "What do you know about that?" Tony asks. The sick feeling rises in him once again.

"Nothing man, I don't know nothing about it," Baine says as his eyes shift towards the window. To his dismay they're still alone.

Tony goes over his mental roster of events — kissing his daughter goodbye before heading off for patrol. She seemed so incredibly happy, more happy than usual. It had been tough for her, losing her mom; but Tony thought on that day that she had finally come through okay. Tony presses his nose closer to Baine's face. "You the fucker who gave my daughter crank?" Baine purses his lips into a tight scowl and shakes his head in the negative. Tony can feel the bag of meth in his pocket pressing against his thigh.

His mind travels back in time, just a few months back coming home to find Lauren lying in her bed surrounded by her favorite teddy bears, her skin ash pale with death, the needle still stuck in her vein and a simple note which read, "I love you daddy."

The sick feeling intensifies as Tony adjusts his grip on the taser. He had never really accepted that his daughter committed suicide, although there was a suicide note. And despite the fact that Lauren had taken a dose of meth so massive that there was no mistaking her death as an accident, Tony still found it hard to believe. No, there had to be someone to blame. He presses the trigger sending an electrical jolt into Baine's neck. Seizing and convulsing Baine lets out a low animal like growl. Tony shocks him again, and then again and again. The more Tony shocks him, the more he feels his own emotional pain. Baine lays limp on the bench, dangling by his cuff. There is some, but not enough satisfaction in harming the boy and then there is the matter of who Baine belongs to and who protects him. Tony steps out of the holding cell and makes his way across the officers' floor. And before leaving the station he flushes the meth down the toilet, one bag which won't make it back on the street, not if he can help it.

***

Keys rattle as the trailer door opens, waking Sunni from her slumber. Still cuffed to the kitchen table's thick legs, she cranes her neck to get a better glimpse of Tony; but all she can see is the underside of his long nostrils as he unfastens his duty belt and plops it on the table.

"Can I go home?" Sunni asks.

Tony grabs a bottle of scotch and a glass tumbler from a high cabinet. He takes a seat at the kitchen table and clears his throat. "You know you can't do that." He pours himself a drink.

"Can you at least take these off me?" Sunni rattles the handcuffs against the table's thick base.

Tony peers down at her. "You run and I'll tie your feet up too." He grabs his cuff keys and unlocks Sunni. Once free, she yanks her hands away but doesn't try to run, she knows that would be futile. Tony kicks out the chair across from him. "Sit down; I want to talk to you," he says. Sunni eases herself into the chair, giving Tony a wary look.

"You hungry?" he asks the girl.

Sunni shrugs her shoulders despite the grumbling in her stomach.

Tony takes a swig of his scotch, avoiding eye contact. He finds the entire situation shameful and just wants to get on with it. "How long have you known Baine?" he finally asks.

Sunni's expression darkens and she hesitantly answers, "I don't really know him."

"You're in his phone."

Sunni is unable to conceal a look of astonishment; she searches his face for any clue of how she was in his phone. "We not friends," she says through tightly clamped teeth.

Tony slumps back in his chair and takes another swig of his drink. He still can't look at Sunni but he's committed to the interrogation. "Did you take those photos at a party or something?"

Sunni's head drops forward and her eyes become watery as studies the tabletop.

"You ashamed now?" Tony takes a huge gulp of his scotch and sits the empty tumbler on the table, "You should be." He pulls Baines' phone out and sits it next to the empty glass. "Wonder how many seen these photos of you? Know how fast an image can travel around the world? To thousands or even millions of people in a minute?"

Sunni stares at the phone. She doesn't need the lecture. She already knows, better than most.

"Is that how your father raised you?" Tony presses his finger pointedly against the phone.

"I don't got no father," Sunni sharply retorts. Her eyes slowly move up the length of Tony's arm stopping at his chin, she can't look him in the eye. No matter how many years passed or how much she wants to, she just can't quite hold her head as high as the rest of the world. "I didn't want to," she mumbles.

Tony is irked by her response. He traces his finger over the back of the phone.

Sunni watches and continues her explanation. "They said nobody here would see them." Not exactly true; but it sounds true enough to tell the cop.

"They?" That word catches Tony's interest. "Baine and some of his thugs?"

Sunni shakes her head. Too many questions.

Tony's eyebrows arch. He waits for his answer, letting an uncomfortable silence enter the space.

"Not him…" Sunni says, her voice trailing off as she once again drops her gaze.

"Who?"

"I don't know."

"You know, tell me."

"I don't know who they are."

"You know their faces."

"I don't know."

Tony's pointed finger transforms into a vice grip on the cell phone, etching the edges of the device into his palm. He shoves the phone back into his pocket and comes to his feet. "You can sleep on the couch," he says as he begins to clear the table. "Tomorrow we'll find you a more permanent home."

Chapter 6

Sunshine peeks through the window of Tony's trailer falling on Sunni's shuttered eyelids; she blinks and slowly rouses from her sleep. Throwing off the blanket and slipping on her sneakers, she gives a long lazy stretch as she peers around the living room and adjacent kitchen. "Officer Gavilan?" she calls out; but there's only silence. Tony's absence surprises her, her instincts tell her that he doesn't trust her, not that she blames him; after all she finds trouble in every city she lives.   She shuffles forward and leans over the couch to take a look out the window. The cruiser is gone, there's only an old silver jalopy in the driveway. The small generator is running, its loud motor roaring. It must be lights out time in this part of the park. Officer Gavilan is one of the lucky ones; most everyone else is shit out of luck when the lights go out for hours. She pivots her head to the right, her grayish blue eyes stopping at family photos, dusty; but lovingly hung on the wall. They're mostly staged snapshots with Tony and Lauren posed for the camera but also some more active images with the entire family, including Tony's deceased wife, the woods offering a scenic backdrop. Sunni turns away from the photos where Tony and his family are all smiles and not the fake kind either. She wonders what it's like to have a truly happy family. She walks through the neat living room and makes her way down the narrow hallway. There are two doors, one to the left and the other to her right. Sunni digs into her pocket and pulls out a penny. She flips the coin. Heads…it's the door to her right. She opens it. The space is tidy, walls dark blue, bed made with black sheets and a satin comforter. She quickly rummages through the drawers; maybe she can find money or an extra set of keys for the jalopy sitting out front. She doesn't find either; but she does find a drawer filled with news clippings, one of which she picks up and examines closer. The headline reads, 'Lauren Gavilan's Death Ruled a Suicide.' The round face seems familiar to Sunni; but she can't quite place her. She looks like the popular type, the kind of girl who wouldn't be interested in associating with someone like her, at least that's how Sunni feels. She glances out the door. Dropping the clipping back into the drawer, she quickly moves into the hallway and towards the other room. She grasps and turns the door knob; but it won't budge. She quickly makes her way into the kitchen and once again goes drawer diving. Finding a small butter knife, she returns to the locked door. She carefully pokes the knife into the keyhole and gives it a hard push popping open the lock. She sits the knife on the floor, turns the knob and smiles as the door opens. A teen girl's dream, walls are adorned with all the latest pop star posters and a dainty framed bed covered in a blanket of teddy bears sits catty corner to an ipod stereo system. She's not exactly sure what she will find but she figures if Lauren was anything like her, she probably had a "cash stash" hidden in the least probable place. And since Lauren is dead, she won't be needing it anymore. Sunni quickly makes her way to the closet, folding back the double doors. "Oh shit!" It is obvious that Lauren dressed well. Sunni thumbs through the clothes, many of which are designer brands. A pang of jealousy hits Sunni's chest, she could never afford anything like that. She peers out the bedroom window to make sure Tony hasn't returned. Once she determines the coast is clear she peels off her old no brand clothing and chooses an outfit she likes. A knee length wool dress embroidered with pink and yellow flowers. She checks herself out in a full length mirror nailed to the back of the door and smiles at the transformation. "Mom was right, clothes do make the person." She grabs her satchel and stuffs it with her old clothes. Finding a pair of knee high white tights and furry boots, she slips them on. As she glances over at the dresser she notices a jewelry box. There could be something worth selling, she tells herself as she opens the jewelry box finding gaudy earrings and a tangle of necklaces. Just as she is about to close the box, she notices something — something shiny. She squints and reaches for it. A silver ring. Sunni frowns and looks at her hand, she's wearing a similar ring, same size and metal. She slips it off and makes a comparison. They are absolutely identical, right down to the inscription, "Never Doubt I Love."

Chapter 7

Tony enters the police station and starts to cross officer's floor; but Carlos is already moving towards him and meets him halfway. "Captain wants to see you," Carlos says with a small grimace. But Tony doesn't look surprised, he knew it was coming so he nods in resignation and makes a b-line for the Captain's office. He knocks on the door. "It's open," Captain Danaski says. Tony turns the knob and enters the office, closing the door behind him. The deep cutting lines over the Captain's brows are the first signs of trouble.

"Have a seat," the Captain says as he swings his feet off the desk and motions towards the empty chair.

Tony obliges, sitting in the sinking soft chair on the other side of the desk. "You wanted to see me, Captain?" he asks.

The Captain presses his elbows onto the desk, the lines on his brow getting deeper as he frowns. "I got a problem, Gavilan."

Tony rests his hands on the arms of the chair, trying to his best to remain calm. The Captain has a way of rattling even the calmest men; but Tony's determined to not fall into that trap. "What's that, Captain?"

"Never knew you to be a hothead," the Captain says.

Tony sighs and starts to say something in his own defense; but he's interrupted.

"I got a kid in holding with stun burns on his skin. You know something about that?" the Captain demands.

The corners of Tony's lips turn downward as he suppresses another sigh. "I was questioning the suspect—"

"I got a 17-year-old kid with fucking burns on his fucking skin, Gavilan," the Captain says, his voice getting louder with each word. "Do you know something about that?"

Tony lets a tense silence linger between them. He hates that tone, condescending at its core. He works hard to suppress his anger. He likes the Captain, in general; but the man could be a tyrant. Tony reaches into his coat pocket and pulls out Baine's phone. He sits it on the desk, letting his hand linger on it for a moment before pulling back and looking the Captain directly in the face. "The suspect was in possession of child pornography," he says.

If anybody was willing to help kids in New Hope, it was the Captain — that he is sure of, even if some of his methods are questionable. The Captain doesn't look at the phone. Instead he silently stares at Tony, his expression deadly serious. But then his serious expression is replaced with a slow rolling smirk and a loud cackle of laughter. It's a reaction Tony isn't prepared for. "Child pornography?" the Captain asks, his torrent of chuckles barely subsiding long enough to speak. "What happened to ya' Tony? When ya' get so soft?" The accusation infuriates Tony; but he just takes it, the Captain is the king of New Hope and the police force his royal court. The Captain leans back in his chair as he continues, "You telling me some hot pants prossies in training sending nudie pics to a knuckleheaded boy is child pornography?" The Captain lets the question sink in; but he's not expecting a response, "This ain't no fucking child pornography. These girls are hot in the pants, that's why they showing their stuff. Don't you get that Gavilan? You can't lock no boy up for that."

Tony grips the arm of his chair. His face is a poker mask and his gaze glued to the Captain's neckline. His Lauren wasn't a prossie in training, far from it, and if she did go that route he would never accept that she went willingly. "The suspect had meth...," Tony says. The captain lifts his index finger, interrupting Tony again, "That don't answer why you felt it was all right to fry that boy up like you did. You know that boy got a heart condition? He could've died on account of ya' actions. Imagine what that would've cost the force. Mighty high price to pay for uncool heads."

Tony finally looks the Captain directly in the face. It takes everything in him to resist the urge to argue, he knew when taking the phone that much of nothing would be done about Baine.

The Captain lowers his finger and relaxes. "If you got some real evidence of somebody being forced to do something they don't want — bring it to me and I'll deal with it. But I can't have my officers roughing up kids, even kids who got bad blood — it can't happen."

Tony says nothing for a few moments, contemplating his next move. "The drug charges?" Tony asks. The Captain sighs. "We going to get that boy some counseling."

Tony's jaws tighten. It figures.

The Captain leans in, resting his forearms on the table. "You lucky you still have a job, Gavilan."

Tony tries to hide is dissatisfaction as he reaches out for Baine's phone; but the Captain quickly snatches it up. "I'll take care of this," the Captain says as he stuffs the phone into his pocket.

Tony slowly retracts his hand "All right," he says. He figures it doesn't matter; he had transferred most of the data to an external drive and was careful to remove Lauren's info from the phone. Her suicide had stigmatized her enough. Tony comes to his feet.

"Gavilan?"

"Yeah?"

"Ain't no record of the meth in evidence…"

"Oh?"

"No."

Tony shrugs. "I checked it in." His voice is flat, emotionless and devoid of the rising tide of anger within. The Captain frowns, something in his gut tells him Tony isn't telling the truth; but since so much evidence went missing, he isn't so sure it is Tony who took it. He returns his attention to the computer as Tony turns and exits the office. Tony makes his way back to the open area where several cops focus their attention on him. He looks right back at them, their angry eyes and partial smirks tempt him to confront them; but he doesn't because he has other matters to tend to, for now. Tony quickly makes his way to his desk where Carlos is standing.

"Everything okay?" Carlos asks.

"Yeah, perfect," Tony says as he takes a seat and cranks up his computer.

Carlos slowly sips his cup of coffee. "What's gotten into you?"

Tony doesn't answer, instead he asks, "Were you popular as a kid? You know, in high school. I mean, did you get a lot of the ladies?"

Carlos stops mid sip and places his cup on the desk. "Is this about Baine and the photos?"

"What, everybody knows about it but me?"

"A lot of things going on you choose not to see, Tony."

"What the fuck is that supposed to mean?"

"Nothing man, calm down."

"Don't tell me to fucking calm down!"

Tony gives Carlos a suspicious look. "What do you know about the girls in that phone?"

Carlos raises his hand in a defensive manner. "Leave it alone. Just leave it, Tony. No harm, no foul."

Tony looks around the station and notices he has caught the attention of other officers. Did they all know that Lauren was one of the 'prossies in training?' He lowers his voice. "What our friendship of 15 years worth to you? Tell me what the fuck is going on?" Tony is out of the loop, an outlier in his tribe of law enforcers. While he continues to live in a fantasy of law and order, his world has succumbed to chaos.

"I'm sorry about Lauren; it's not your fault," Carlos says, trying to console him.

Tony slowly swivels his head, narrowed eyes aimed at Carlos. He suspects that Carlos knew that Lauren was one of Baine's girls. After fifteen years of friendship and a crap load of favors, Carlos didn't even have the decency to tell him the ugly truth and give his daughter a chance, a thought which infuriates Tony. He springs to his feet. And in one fiery motion of rage he punches Carlos in the nose sending the man sprawling onto the floor. For five years he had watched as the department went from one that protects, to one that ignores and eventually to one that corrupts. He thought he could build a fortress around his Lauren but he failed. Not only had he failed but he didn't see what was happening right under his nose. He towers over Carlos as the man writhes on the stained concrete floor, his fists ready to pound into him again; but just as he's giving it another go, several officers rush in, hold him back, tackle him to the ground and inflict a retributory beating of their own.

Chapter 8

The building at 532 Main Street was once a luxury condominium complex. The pride of New Hope, the building had five floors of luxurious condos with sunken tubs, Jacuzzis and balconies overlooking the city and forest that surrounds it on the western border. Everyone who was anyone wanted to live CityScape's promise that they could enjoy small town living with big city amenities. It was the New York of the south, advertisements boasted. But now the building is only a shadow of its former self. Wealthy residents fled long ago or were cast into the sea of the unmoneyed masses once their fortunes soured. Sunni never knew the building's former glory nor does she care, her mind only focuses on keeping her footing steady as she walks over the dust covered wooden floor. Sporadic holes in the ceiling spill sunlight into the hallway. "Which way...," Sunni mutters to herself as she glances down yet another hallway. There's a sound, one that stands out amongst the constant groans and creaks of the dilapidated structure. She freezes, her muscles tighten and her eyes search for the source of the distinct noise. A round man carrying a shotgun emerges from one of the apartments, his eyes fixed on Sunni. "What you want?!" he demands as he raises his gun, aiming the barrel at Sunni's midsection.

Sunni slowly raises her hands, not quite able to find the right words for a response that won't leave her dead.

There's a glimmer of recognition in the man's eyes. The man lowers his gun; but only slightly. "You coming to settle up?"

Sunni quickly shakes her head, her hands still raised. "Looking for my mom."

"Well she ain't checked in and she ain't settled up," the shot gun wielding man says.

Sunni tries to peer into the apartment from which the man emerged; but he closes the door.

"I got business to tend to kid, so if you ain't checking in and you ain't settling up, then ya' trespassing. And I don't take too kindly to that." He raises his gun again.

Sunni averts her gaze but she doesn't leave. "You know where she went?"

The man frowns. "Where she went? She ain't' been around for a few days." He pauses for a moment, then asks, "When you last seen her?" He studies the girl.

Sunni is quiet sensing she has said too much, her mother's words 'loose lips sink ships,' ring in her ears. "I'm going to leave," Sunni says as she takes a step backwards.

The man cocks his gun. "She owe me a lot of cash." He hadn't seen the woman in more than a week; but he hadn't thought much of it. He had given her enough meth to get by on and she always paid on time before, so when she let a day lapse without payment he hadn't become too nervous.

A shiver of terror runs through Sunni as she stares down the barrel of the gun. The man quickly steps forward. She tries to run away. He grabs her wrist. She struggles. But he's too strong. She's shoved into the apartment and the door and slammed shut behind them.

The apartment is stuffed with junk. The kitchen counters, tables and floors are covered with Pyrex baking dishes, hot plates, soiled soda bottles and mason jars filled with various liquids. A slender teenage boy sits behind a table cluttered with mason jars and surgical tubing, his mouth and nose covered with a camo bandana. He quickly comes to his feet and his eyes widen as Sunni is dragged further into the apartment.

"Let me go!" Sunni lands a few futile kicks on the man's shin.

The teenage boy slowly pulls the bandana down, revealing his face — it's Jin.

"Help me!" Sunni calls out to the boy. But Jin doesn't move. He shifts his gaze from Sunni to the man. "What she doing here?"

The man's expression grows stern. "I'm needing to answer to you now?"

Jin shifts his eyes downward; of course the man doesn't need to answer to him at all. He only looks up again when Sunni is shoved into a chair and given a few violent shakes.

"Shut the fuck up now," the man growls as he shakes her. Sunni stops struggling and the man points to Jin. "That boy right there gonna' show you everything you need to know." He redirects his finger to the space between Sunni's eyes. "Just do what ya' told and we'll get you home in no time."

Sunni struggles to breathe through the panic. "You can't keep me here...."

Jin shakes his head and frowns. He can't help but speak up again. "You going to have her cooking?"

The man gives Jin another stern look. He doesn't like being questioned, especially by some kid. But he entertains him anyway. "Got a rush on this order for Lucky cause Baine had a loss," the man says as he slowly stands upright and steps away from Sunni. Baine had a loss and the girl's no good mama owes him a shitload of cash. Seems like a situation that can work out good for all involved.

Jin frowns a bit. "I got to share my cut?" He needs the money and doesn't want share any of it and he certainly doesn't want to be replaced.

The man adjusts his gun. "I got to answer twenty questions from you now?"

Jin lowers his gaze again and mumbles, "If she ain't cooked before it could be dangerous."

"That's why you here," the man says as he turns and walks towards the apartment door, "to teach her. Ain't that hard…they're two of ya'. I'm expecting it done in half the time." He opens the door and steps into the hallway.

Jin pulls the bandana back over his nose and mouth as the door is partially closed. "This is dangerous work," he says as if his work is something he's proud of.

Sunni glances around the room and towards a window — no fire escape — too high up.

"Start with something small," Jin says.

Sunni spins back around, her suspicious gaze falling on Jin as he points to a liquid filled plastic Coke bottle. "Grab that bottle there and give it a good shake…," he says. He notices the suspicious gaze. "Sorry about what happened the other day…," he adds. He doesn't look her in the eye, he feels ashamed for having not done more; but at the same time, he accepts that it's just the way things are.

Sunni cautiously grabs the Coke bottle and gives a hesitant answer, "Thanks for giving me my coat back and not…not telling 'em you saw me." She doesn't know what to make of the boy, but she needs as many friends as she can get. She gently shakes the bottle, letting her gaze drift towards the apartment entrance.

Jin's eyes brighten, "I couldn't fit it no way." He follows her gaze, "Need to give it a good shake."

Sunni looks at him again as she shakes the bottle more. "You think you'd mind helping me get outta here?"

Jin shakes his head and grabs another empty Coke bottle. "That ain't possible." He pours some liquid into it and replaces the cap.

Sunni shrinks with disappointment and shakes the bottle more vigorously.

"Make sure that cap is on tight," Jin warns. Sunni stops her shaking and tries to tighten the top; but Jin grabs the soda bottle and gives the cap another twist. "You'll get the hang of it," he says, his eyes pleasant but weary.

"You don't seem like one of Baine's boys," Sunni says, a bit surprised by his kindness.

"Well I ain't exactly."

"You hang with him."

Jin frowns and nods. "Just to get by for now." He organizes the white pills in a clear bowl. "You Sunni right?" he asks her.

She nods and coughs on the stench of rotten eggs, her body already showing the ill effects of the toxic fumes. Jin adjusts his bandana. "Don't got an extra covering but maybe you can use toilet paper," he whispers, trying to make sure the man with the shotgun can't hear him. He jerks his head to the right and comes to his feet. He motions for Sunni to follow him past the slightly ajar door where the shotgun man talks on the phone in the hallway.

"Shipment gone is what Baine said....Ain't no getting his money back....It ain't my problem..." shotgun man barks into the phone as the duo sneak past and enter the bathroom.

The bathroom is filthy, more like an outhouse than anything. Sunni frowns hard at the conditions.

"I just hold it," Jin chuckles.

"What's gonna' happen to me?" Sunni doesn't bother with trying to be tough, her fear is obvious.

Jin pulls down his bandana revealing dry blackened lips, "He ain't a bad guy, just wanting you to settle up is all, like he said. He ain't gonna mess with ya' or nothing if that's what you worried about."

A blush of red rushes Sunni's cheeks at Jin's suggestion. "Wasn't saying that, just want to get on out of here and on my way," she clarifies. "Don't like being locked up."

Jin begins to unravel a roll of toilet paper. "Well guess the faster we get this done; the faster we both get out of here." He layers the strips of toilet paper. "Hold this," he orders the girl. Sunni uses her fingers to pin the ends near each of her ears.

"You got something to hold that in your hair?" Jin asks.

Sunni shakes her head.

Jin searches the drawers and the medicine cabinet where he finally finds a large overstretched rubber band. He loops it around her forehead and to the back of her neck making her giggle.

"I don't want to look stupid." Of all the things she has to worry about, she still worries about her appearance.

Jin laughs. "Thought somebody wid' a name like Sunni be use to that," he says.

"What's that suppose to mean?"

"Don't mean nothing, just different is all."

"No it ain't," Sunni huffs indignantly.

"Didn't mean to hurt ya' feelings."

"Didn't hurt my feelings. Anyway, it ain't no more stupider than Gin. What ya' mama was a drunk or something when she had ya'?"

Jin frowns offering no response. He walks past her, stepping out of the bathroom and making his way back to his table. Sunni stands in the bathroom alone. After a few moments she finally joins him. "Sorry...I ain't gonna' say it twice," Sunni sputters out as she stands over Jin. And she frowns as he drops a handful of white pills into a mason jar. She offers further explanation. "I'm sure ya' mama a nice person and all and don't take too much of the strong stuff," she concludes. Jin sits the jar aside and peers up from his work. His voice flat and cold, he says, "I never met her." Eyes on the white pills again. "She offed herself."

Sunni looks away regretfully. "Sorry, I...."

"Thought you said you not gonna' say it twice."

Sunni stops and looks back at him, confused when she sees a smile.

"I don't know her no way, never did...just that...well never imagined she'd be drinking gin is all," Jin says with an easy grin. Laughter pours out of the teens as they consider the comical image of Jin's unknown mother getting drunk right in the middle of popping out Jin.

"Take that there," — Jin points to a gallon sized white and green bottle — "and pour a little of it in that coke bottle just like how I show ya' earlier."

Sunni lifts the container and unscrews the cap. She takes a little sniff and immediately begins to cough, a burning sensation in her nostrils and throat.

"Not like that!" Jin yells.

An involuntary jerky movement sends an eruption of a clear watery substance onto Sunni's arms and face and within a few seconds she's screaming as her skin burns and peels off. Jin runs around the table and grabs the emergency jug of water — it's only half full. Someone has been drinking it. He douses Sunni with what remains in the jug and rushes to the kitchen sink. Pray to God that there is water in the pipeline. Didn't he say there was water in the pipeline? Sunni's screams continues. The searing heat is unbearable, like someone doused her with gasoline and struck a match. The round man rushes into the room. "What the hell is going on here?!" he yells over Sunni's screams.

His gaze falls on Sunni trembling on the ground. "Aww fuck!" He has his own emergency stash of water. He grabs the jug and douses Sunni with it. But it's not enough; and it is only unconsciousness that offers Sunni the relief she needs.

***

Wrapped in a dark blue blanket, Sunni whimpers in the bed of the pickup truck as it stops in front of Tony's trailer. "Help me get her out," the round man says as he makes his way to the back of the truck. Jin follows him. Together they lift Sunni out of the truck's bed and carry her to the trailer's porch. She cries out as their fingers press against the fresh burns which seem to get worse by the minute.

"Alright, sit her down," the round man says.

"What? You mean we gonna' just leave her here?" Jin asks as he carefully lowers Sunni to the ground.

"What ya' have me do? Explain myself?"

The round man lowers Sunni to the cold concrete and all but runs back to the truck. Jin raps the door hard before racing back to the truck and jumping into the passenger's seat. He's barely pulled his leg in before the truck takes off. Jin cranes his neck to look at the trailer, hoping someone opens the door. He's relieved when he finally sees the shadow of a man standing over Sunni.

Already dressed in pajamas and a robe, Tony stands over Sunni with his gun drawn and ready. He looks down to see Sunni laying on the porch and crying. He isn't expecting that. He kneels beside her, examining her red face for a moment before trying to lift her. She lets out another anguished cry. He gently sits her down again and carefully unwraps the blanket, unmasking a splash of chemical burns on the girl's arms. He quickly bundles her into his arms and rushes her into the warmth of the trailer.

Chapter 9

Darkness is all Sunni sees when she wakes up. She's startled as she feels someone touch her hand.

"Patches come off soon," the man touching her hand says. Sunni doesn't recognize the voice but she does have a vague recollection of the same voice saying soothing things to her over a disjointed timeframe she can't quite sort out.

"Where am I?" she asks.

"At my house."

"Who?

"Officer Gavilan."

Sunni sinks deeper into the bed as she tries to slide her hand away from Tony.

"Please let me go," she says, her voice is weak and scared.

"Can't go until you all healed up," Tony says, trying hard to keep an even and hopefully soothing tone.

"Why can't I see nothing?"

"Them patches come off soon enough," he repeats.

Sunni tries to lift her arms but Tony stops her. "Burns got to heal first."

She struggles to lift her arms again; but Tony takes hold of them, stopping all movement. "Am I ugly?" Sunni asks.

Tony shakes his head although she can't see it. "Keep doing that, the longer it will take to heal up," he says as he watches her lips crumple, something his daughter also once did whenever he inadvertently hurt her feelings. He sighs and softens his voice a little more. "Your face going to heal up just fine. They had the decency to at least wash that crap off …but your eyes…."

Sunni's breathing quickens and she tries even harder to see. Tony lays a gentle hand on her forehead and offers reassurance, "Doctor says it'll be fine most likely. Depend on how deep it went in; but we don't think it went in too far."

Sunni turns her head to the side, her body trembling. Tony pulls the blanket up to her shoulders and heads towards the door passing the double closet, the ipod stereo still in place but the posters and teddy bears gone.

"Get some rest," he says, standing in the doorway. He flicks off the lights.

***

Sunni's back rests against the headboard, the eye patches gone. She places her right hand over her right eye. "T O Z," she says as she reads off the letters from the eye chart. "Uhm...I think that's an I." She sighs in frustration and lowers her hand.

Tony rolls up the eye chart and slides it into a drawer. "Better than last week, right?" he asks.

Sunni nods, it is much better. At least she can see. "I'm gonna' have to wear thick glasses?"

The comment makes Tony smile a little. "Don't worry about that right now."

"Surprised you ain't sent me to fostering."

Tony closes the drawer and rests his hand on the knob. "Thought you didn't want to go."

"Thought you wanted me to go."

Tony turns to face the girl, taking in her red but healing skin and the dark circles around her eyes. "Let's cross that bridge when we get to it." He grabs a dropper off the dresser top and walks towards the bed, "Tilt your head back and don't blink until after." Sunni cringes but obeys.

***

Sunni sits on the couch flicking through the television channels every five seconds. Tony comes out of his bedroom stretching.

"Thought you was gonna' sleep all day," Sunni says, her gaze glued to the television.

Tony pauses and gives the girl a look of annoyance, then makes his way towards the fridge.

"We outta booze," Sunni says as she continues her channel flipping.

Tony redirects his steps towards the cabinets. Sunni turns to watch him.

"Keep your eyes on that television," Tony warns.

Sunni quickly spins around and focuses on the TV.

"You do your exercises?" Tony asks as he digs into the space under the sink.

Sunni lifts and bends her arm in a flippy floppy fashion while making rolling her eyes.

"Okay now, don't complain to me when you can't move your arms properly," he says as he pulls a bottle of scotch from under the sink.

"Why you don't work no more?" Sunni asks.

The question causes Tony to pause for a moment. He looks at the back of Sunni's head as she continues to fiddle with the remote. He lets out a low level groan and grabs a glass tumbler. "Come here," he says as he pours himself a drink.

Sunni hops off the couch and shuffles towards the kitchen, the skin on her face is mostly free of red blotches but her arms are still badly scarred.

"Why don't you go and put some food in that mouth of yours and mind the business on your TV programs," Tony says.

Sunni lowers her gaze, sheepishly walks to the fridge and opens it. She can feel Tony's eyes on her back as she grabs a gallon of milk and a box of kiddie cereal and she can smell the sharp scent of the alcohol as she takes a seat and pours herself a bowl of cereal.

"Forgot something?" Tony asks as he pulls a spoon from the dish rack and hands it to her. She takes it, avoids eye contact and slowly stirs the cereal.

"It don't taste good soggy," he warns her.

Sunni nods and slowly lifts a spoonful of cereal to her lips.

Silence lingers between them as Tony gulps his scotch and continues watching her.

"Something wrong?" she asks.

"Nope."

Sunni lifts her eyes just a little and quickly lowers them when she notices he is still staring at her.

"Actually," Tony says as he finally looks away. "Was wondering if you're ready to talk about what happened."

Sunni finally lifts her eyes fully, a bit surprised. "But I did tell ya'."

He shifts his gaze to her once again. "That's not what I'm talking about," he says.

Sunni lowers her head.

"Is this how it's going to be?" Tony asks.

Sunni gives no response.

Tony gulps down the rest of his drink and pours another. "Maybe you better off in foster care," he says.

Sunni looks up, the hurt in her eyes unmistakable.

Tony avoids looking at her. He clears his throat and takes a very large gulp of his drink. "Just saying," he says. "If I'm going to help you, you got to help me...help you."

Her eyes on the bowl of cereal again, Sunni speaks up timidly, "I don't...."

"Let's start with the pictures in the phone...who took them?"

"I don't know...all of 'em."

"Thought you said you didn't know none?"

"I know one."

"Who?"

"Baine's dad."

Tony's grip tightens on the bottle of scotch, "Who else?"

"Don't know."

"Know their face?"

"Maybe."

"What you get for it?"

"Nothing."

"That ain't what I hear."

Sunni slowly lifts her gaze to study Tony's face. "What you hear?" she asks.

"I hear you whoring yourself out," he says bluntly.

"I ain't no whore!"

"When you sell your body for money that makes you a whore," Tony gulps down the rest of his drink and walks to the kitchen sink. He rinses the glass tumbler and sits it in the dish rack.

Sunni's face reddens. She bites down on her lip as her eyes moisten.

"You do it for that ring?" Tony asks, he considers it a cheap price; but he considers the possibility anyway.

"What?"

Tony turns again to face her. "The ring," he says.

Sunni glances at her finger and finds the silver ring is missing. "I'm sorry I took her ring," she says, remembering the ring she found in Lauren's jewelry box.

Tony's expression hardens; he turns again towards the sink and grabs the glass tumbler again. He had seen Lauren wearing that ring numerous times; but he never questioned it. Why didn't he question it? The thought of it makes him feel sick to his stomach. Returning to the table he pours himself another drink, anything to quell the sick feeling rising within him. "Who gave you that ring?" he asks.

"I found it," she lies.

Tony studies her face as he takes another long gulp of his scotch. "A big coincidence? A coincidence that you and my daughter have the same rings?"

Sunni nods, "Yeah, I guess so."

"Right," he slams the empty glass on the table. He doesn't believe for one moment that it's a coincidence; but at the same time he hopes that he's wrong. He comes to his feet and sits the glass in the sink. "Got work to do," he says. "I suspect you'll be here when I get back."

Sunni gives a quick nod making sure to avoid looking at him as he heads to his bedroom to get ready for his patrol.

***

Tony enters the pawn shop, its bright lights "Buy Sell Pawn" blinking despite the fact that it's the middle of the day. The clerk, an older, balding man wearing a grey sweatshirt, leans on the glass case. "How can I help ya' officer?" the clerk asks. Tony sits two silver rings on the glass case, "These look familiar?"

The pawn shop clerk slips on his eyeglasses and examines the rings, "Can't say right off. Got a lot of things coming through here...When did you get it?"

Tony frowns as he thinks back to when he first noticed the silver ring on his daughter and regrets not asking about it at the time. He was so busy then, always busy. "About a good six or eight months back I think? Can you check your books?" he asks.

"Don't know if we keep 'em that far back...the station may have 'em," the clerk says and walks to the back room.

"Now you know they don't keep up with papers too well, much less anything else," Tony says with a forced smile.

The man lets out a low chuckle as he glances back at Tony. "Now ain't that the truth," the clerk says. He grabs a black three-ring binder and returns to the glass case. He thumbs through a few pages and shakes his head. "I got a few silver rings here..." — he looks at the two rings again — "But...well I don't know about the engraving...could have been added...but I ain't for sure." He sits the rings back down. "You need these pages here?"

"That would be good," Tony says.

"I'll just make a copy for ya'," the clerk says as he removes three pages and then disappears into the back room again.

Tony collects the rings and stuffs them back into his pocket as the chugging sound of the copier emanates from the back room. "Who around here does engraving?" Tony asks.

"Josh's daddy...What's his name?...Mikey...You know Mikey? He used to do it some, up there on Troy Street. But ain't did it since he close up shop. Ain't many folks doing engraving no more," the clerk says as he returns with the copies.

Tony takes the copies, folds them and stuffs them into his jacket's inner pocket, "You know where Mikey staying about now?"

"Hear he still holding on to that house up there on Chandler Road."

Tony nods, "Thanks for your help." He backs up and heads for the shop door. But as Tony is leaving, Lucky Robbie swiftly makes his way into the pawn shop. His tall lean body lightly brushes against Tony as if he doesn't even see him.

Tony tenses and instinctively grabs the man by the collar. Lucky yanks away and gives him a get the fuck off me look. "Help you officer?" Lucky demands as Tony removes his hand. "Talk to you for a minute? Outside...," Tony says as he motions towards the door. He really wants to bash his head in and leave the man for dead in a back alley; but he's still a man of the law so he resists the urge. "Talk right here," Lucky says wanting witnesses if anything goes wrong. The pawn shop clerk watches nervously and starts to back up and leave. "Where you going?" Lucky asks without even looking to see that the clerk was trying to sneak off. "That how you treat customers?" he asks as he turns to look at the clerk.

Tony steps closer to Lucky. "Only fucking customer you're going to be is the customer of some shit pusher in the state pen when I'm through with you," he says, the corner of his lips reaching down towards his jaw line. He's convinced that Lucky had something to do with the rings and the death of his daughter. "Coming to get another set of rings? Or you looking for these?" he pulls out the rings and shows them to Lucky. Lucky keeps a straight face and shakes his head. "Don't know what you talking about," he says and tries to walk towards the counter.

"Don't you fucking walk away from me…," Tony starts but is interrupted by Lucky.

"You here to arrest me for something…or you just pissing in the wind." Lucky is arrogant now, he knows that if Tony had an arrest warrant he would be in handcuffs already. Tony doesn't say anything, but he doesn't stand down nor does he break his glare. Lucky smirks and continues towards the counter, his back to Tony, "I didn't think so." He stops and turns towards Tony again, "Don't think I den' forgot what you did to my boy…," his glare matching Tony's hate filled gaze. "You'll be hearing from my lawyer…," he says sarcastically.

"Yeah? Well I hope he's got a good defense for child pornography," Tony says. He knows he has no case, not because there is no actual case but because no one really cares enough to pursue it. Lucky just laughs and turns his back to Tony. Tony pushes open the pawn shop door and heads out to the street. He doesn't head back to the police station; but immediately heads towards the grocery store which is less than a block away. Tony steps into Raj's grocery store and immediately goes for the alcohol section. "Evening officer," Raj says as Tony passes him. Picking up a bottle of scotch and a case of beer, Tony gives a distracted wave. Raj watches him and starts with his weekly complaints, "Got lots of problems this week with punks…." Tony tunes him out as he makes his way towards the dairy section and picks up a dozen eggs and a gallon of milk and heads back to the counter.

"Give me a pack," Tony says, as he points towards the cigarette case. Raj grabs a case of cigarettes and looks at Tony's other items curiously as he rings them up. The eggs catch his attention. "Thought you didn't touch that stuff officer," he says. Tony grabs the pack of cigarettes and lights one right there in the store. "Not for me…," he says.

"Oh…," Raj nods and tries to not cough on the smoke.

Tony looks at him and asks, "You got kids?"

Raj is surprised at this question, Tony never really asks Raj anything about himself. "Yes sir, have four of my own," he tells him and he nods and grins at the thought but he feels empathy for the loss of Tony's child.

Tony blows out the smoke and says, "Never knew that…teen girls?"

Raj nods, "Yes sir, I got two, thirteen and sixteen…"

"Go to New Hope High?"

Raj frowns and says, "No…not there…uhm another school…we work hard to get them in private school."

Tony nods again. "Yeah smart." He pays for the food and tucks the bag under his arm. "They got friends…boyfriends…," he continues his interrogation.

Raj's response is curt and quick, "No." He doesn't know what Tony is getting at, so he adds, "They are good girls," emphasizing the word good.

"Of course they are," Tony says and takes a long puff on his smoke. He blows out a stream of smoke for what seems like a lengthy ten seconds. "You have a good one," he finally says and heads out of the shop.

***

Sunni stares out the window of the trailer watching the rooftop icicles melt. Her gaze sometimes shifts to the road. She still holds onto the hope that her mom will come looking for her; but it's been two months since the woman took off. Her mind drifts to her ever present worry — what's next? The ringing of a phone interrupts her contemplation. She turns away from the window. Following the sound of the ringing she finds her cell phone on the end table by the couch. She quickly answers, "Hello…." She stops breathing for a moment as she listens to the voice on the other end. "I didn't mean nothing by it…," she says. "I didn't have nothing to do with that….No….No….I don't want to…." She bites her nails as she continues to press the phone against her ear, "I'm all ugly now…." She jumps as the voice booms through the receiver, "I didn't mean too….You don't even know what happened…." She continues to nibble her nails and shift her eyes nervously, "But you said…but you promised I ain't got to do that no more…You promised!"

She disconnects the call and comes to her feet pacing the living room floor, biting her nails and worrying. She had hoped that she had been forgotten; but obviously that was wishful thinking. She looks at her phone again and then smashes it on the floor as hard as she can. But it doesn't break. She picks it up again and frantically tries to dismantle it, but that fails too and then the phone starts to ring again. She rejects the call. In a full scale panic, she runs to the bathroom dropping the phone into the toilet bowl and flushing repeatedly. The swish of water masks the sound of the trailer door opening. Sunni grabs the plunger and shoves the stick into the toilet, pressing against the phone as she flushes.

"What are you doing?" Tony's voice is stern.

Sunni spins around to find Tony standing in the doorway of the bathroom scowling at her as the toilet completes another unsuccessful flush.

He pushes her aside and eyes the telephone in the toilet bowl. After giving her another look, he plucks it out of the toilet. Beads of sweat cover Sunni's face as she watches him.

He tips the phone on its side letting a stream of water pour out and gives her a strange look. He tries to turn on the phone but it doesn't work. "Get the hair dryer," Tony says.

"It's okay...," Sunni says, trying to back away.

"Just do what I say," Tony says.

Sunni backs up and hesitantly goes into the bedroom. Grabbing the hair dryer, she returns to the bathroom and hands it to Tony.

Tony opens the phone and blow dries the components as Sunni watches him nervously.

"Why were you trying to flush your phone down the toilet?" Tony asks, his voice loud over the sound of the hair dryer.

"I wasn't...it was an accident," Sunni speaks just as loud to compete with the dryer's roar.

Tony stops blow drying. "I sat there and watched you flushing over and over, Sunni," he says as he sits the dismantled phone on the washbasin.

Sunni's gaze searches his face as if she might find something there, some inkling of his suspicions. She tilts her right foot on its side as she tries to come up with an answer — the truth or a fabrication.

"He called me again," Sunni says.

"Lucky?"

"No...," Sunni says as she looks away from Tony.

Tony seems surprised by her answer. "Who then?"

"You ain't gonna' believe me."

"Try me."

Sunni watches the deep lines in his forehead caused by his severe frown and seriousness. In the two months she's been living with Tony, that frown sometimes gave way to a smile or even a grin and it was at those moments that she liked and trusted the man the most. But then there are times like now, times when he gives her a threatening look, that she fears him and wishes to be someplace else. She lowers her gaze.

"I don't know his real name," she says.

Tony begins to reassemble the phone. "Why wouldn't I believe that?" he asks.

"Cause you said I'm a liar and you don't believe nothing I say."

"You ain't been lying?" Tony asks. He had been catching her in several lies, a fact that made him distrust her even more than he did before.

Sunni doesn't respond.

"What's the name you got?" Tony asks.

Sunni is quiet for a long time, long enough to rile Tony's impatience.

"What ya'—" he starts.

"Candy Man," Sunni says quickly before Tony can get even angrier with her.

Tony narrows his gaze at her. "Candy Man?" He's never heard of anyone named that in New Hope.

Sunni nods.

Tony finishes reassembling the phone but it still doesn't turn on. "There's no Candy Man," he says. "When you going to start telling me the truth?"

Sunni shifts nervously, bouncing her right foot up and down, her slight frame even smaller before Tony's tall, muscular body. She slowly lifts her eyes to meet his gaze. It was something she had mulled over for weeks; but now she's sure of it. "I knew your daughter...well, knew of her...," she says.

Tony's voice goes from stern to raspy, "What?..."

"Knew she was in that phone...."

Tony says nothing, he only stares at the girl trying to take it all in and figure out what it means that his daughter knew the "prossie in training."

"He did it to her too...."

"What?" Tony finds himself temporarily speechless and unable to figure out Sunni's angle.

"She was just like me...," Sunni continues, nervously fidgeting with her fingers.

"My daughter was nothing like you...," Tony says with enough venom to give Sunni a sinking feeling; but the girl continues anyway.

"Yes she was ...," Sunni says.

"What type of game you playing?" Tony asks as he narrows his eyes further and gives Sunni a piercing look.

Sunni shakes her head. "I'm not...."

"Your mother put you up to this?"

Sunni shakes her head even harder. "No...."

"You come on to me...now you telling me my daughter was like you...," Tony says, his anger slowing growing into hatred. How dare her soil Lauren's name.

Sunni lowers her head, offering herself to Tony still brings shame every time she thinks about it, "I didn't want to go to fostering...," she says, that was why she did it.

"That your plan now...tell me a bunch of lies so you ain't got to go?"

he asks, his voice raising as he grasps her arm roughly. "Well you get the hell out of my house!" He tries to pull her out of the bathroom.

Sunni resists and yells out, "The Captain…it was the Captain."

"What?" His vice grip tightens.

"The Captain…he was the one…."

"You're fucking lying!" He has his issues with the Captain; but Sunni's accusations are unbelievable.

"No! I'm not!"

Tony continues to drag her down the hallway and towards the living room. He doesn't know what type of game she's playing but her accusation against the Captain is the last straw. Sunni pulls back, not wanting to go, at least not until she has some type of solid plan for surviving on her own.

"I can prove it! I can prove…he has a birthmark! Right here," she says as she points to her inner thigh, her hand trembling.

Tony stops pulling for a moment. He tries to remember if he had seen a birthmark on the Captain. He isn't sure.

"It's the truth!" Sunni says, hoping she can convince him that she's telling the truth. And the look on his face gives her hope that she's broken through…at least a little. And she has broken through, a flood of doubt enters Tony's mind.

Chapter 10

Tony's left hand presses down on the Captain's desk as he tosses the two rings on the leather placemat. The Captain glances at the rings and smiles. "Your daughter...," he says.

Tony tenses and his eyes widen as he wonders if the man has so much power that he feels no need to hide the truth.

The Captain picks up one of the rings and looks at it. "If she had only taken my advice," he says.

Confusion replaces Tony's outrage. He had been wanting to kill the captain for days once he convinced himself that he was somehow involved in the death of his daughter. But now that he is face-to-face with the man, his doubts rise again. He doesn't really want to believe it anyway. He has his differences with the Captain; but this was the man who was there for him when he most needed him. Could it really be true that he would hurt his daughter?

The Captain sighs and hands Tony the ring. "You should keep this...it was a gift," he says.

Tony frowns, still looking confused. He doesn't take the ring. "Why you give my daughter a ring?" he asks.

Now it's the Captain's turn to be confused. "It's a purity ring. I give them to all the girls," he says.

Tony's expression softens. "Purity ring?"

"Just my way of protecting 'em is all...," the Captain says. He sighs again. "Don't always work." He slides the ring across the desk towards Tony.

Tony is shocked and unsure of how to process this new piece of information.

The Captain studies Tony's expression. "I let you down...I'm sorry," he says.

Stunned by the Captain's apology, Tony suddenly feels guilty for jumping to conclusions. He picks up the rings. "It's not your fault," he says, his face burning from embarrassment; but he also feels relieved that he doesn't need to go through on his plan. He frowns again as he thinks of Sunni — she seemed so convincing. Maybe the Captain is right — can't trust prossies in training; but then again what about his own daughter? It it true that she knew Sunni?

Was she really one of Baine's girls? He doesn't want to believe it. He can't reconcile what he knew of his daughter with the reality he's being presented.

"You fostering now?" the Captain asks.

Jolted out of his own thoughts, Tony is surprised by the question. But he doesn't really know why he's surprised; nothing is secret for too long in New Hope.

"Just looking after her till her mom gets back," Tony says.

The Captain nods. "She's trouble…" the Captain says with a frown. "Might want to be careful… I tried to help that one; but…" — He shakes his head — "Fruit don't fall far from the tree."

Tony is suddenly concerned, maybe Sunni was yanking his chain and manipulating him; but it seemed so real.

"You do know about the tree…right?" the Captain asks.

Tony nods. "Of course." He wonders what he doesn't know; but he's not willing to make a fool out of himself by asking.

"You're a good man, Tony," the Captain says. "Let me know if you need anything, anything at all."

Tony is confused and unsettled by the turn events. A part of him wants to believe that the Captain is telling the truth; but another part of him feels that something is not right. But he senses that there is something that he doesn't know.

Tony nods and shoves the rings back into his pocket. "Did you know Lauren was using meth?" he asks bluntly.

The Captain frowns hard and shakes his head. "No…I didn't."

Tony sighs. "She trusted you…more than she did me…." He turns towards the door.

The Captain nods as Tony starts to walk out the door and adds, "She's not Lauren…she can't replace your daughter, Tony."

Tony turns to look at the Captain again. "You think you got to tell me that?" Tony scoffs at the thought; but he admits only to himself that he sees Sunni as his chance to make amends to Lauren.

"There's no case, you know," the Captain continues.

Tony cocks his head to the side with curiosity. What does he mean by that?

"Don't think I don't know about you snooping around trying to get information about those rings. What? You were going to come in here and rough me up like how you roughed up Baine — and Carlos?"

Tony looks away partly humiliated that his intentions were transparent; but also wondering why the Captain was snooping around on him. "You don't trust me?" he asks.

"You been through a rough patch. I'm looking out for you."

"By snooping on me?"

"Your daughter…she was a good kid…just got in with the wrong people, that's all…that's nobody's fault," the Captain says.

Tony doesn't want to hear it; he turns away and fights back the wave of grief.

"She's gone Tony, she ain't coming back…," the Captain continues.

Tony looks at him again with an anguished and annoyed expression. "Don't you think I know that? Don't you think I live with it every day?"

The Captain raises his hand to interrupt Tony, "Nobody's to blame that's all I'm saying. She got in with the wrong people and…well, she lost herself…but this girl Sunni, she may have a second chance. That's what you're thinking, right?"

Tony stares at him, wondering why he wanted to know. "I don't know…just uhm…can't find anyone to keep her…town full of folks who can't be bothered with a teenager," he says as he remembers Mrs. Danaski's reaction to Sunni. "Must of caused trouble for your wife?"

The Captain looks surprised. "Trouble?" Genuinely confused he says, "Not that I know of…."

"That's funny…"

"What?"

"Well, the missus didn't seem too fond of Sunni at all…it's strange cause I know she loves just about every kid in this town no matter how rotten," he says with a strained chuckle.

And for the first time in the conversation the Captain pales. "I'll have to look into that."

Tony studies his reaction noting the sudden change.

"The missus has been having some issues lately…with her age and all…you know…that thing…not my place to mention it really but just want ya' to let Sunni know it's not personal," the Captain says.

Tony furrows his brow. "Right…it's not personal," he agrees and then he turns to leave again; but the Captain's next question stops him.

"Did Sunni mention why she thought the missus was acting strange?" the Captain asks.

Tony looks over his shoulder at the Captain, "No, she said she never met her before."

The Captain looks relieved. "Yeah, they've never met, not that I know of…but I'm sure they'll get to at the Easter bash," he laughs and smiles widely.

Tony nods and exits the room mulling over everything again as he makes his way across the station and out to start his patrol.

***

Tony's police cruiser pulls up in front of the trailer. The car window is rolled down to let in the warm Spring air. Tony pops the trunk and hops out of the car, holding a 12 pack of beer and smoking a cigarette.

"Sunni!" he calls out, sounding harsher than he wants.

Sunni comes to the trailer door. "Yeah...," she says. The door half open, she lingers at the top of the trailer's concrete porch, her long black hair bunched into a ponytail and her jeans rolled up to the knee.

"Got something in the trunk for ya'," Tony says as he tucks the pack of beer under his arm and blows out a plume of smoke.

Sunni grins, she always looks forward to getting things. And despite Tony's curmudgeon nature he always seems to think of her when shopping. She quickly makes her way down the stairs and walks past Tony. Lifting the hood of the half open trunk and she takes a peep and finds her scraggily puppy scampering about, it's a lot taller; but also thin looking and bit mangier than usual. "Sasha!" Sunni says and scoops the puppy into her arms letting it squirm about and lick her face. She had written the puppy off as another loss; but is delighted that she was wrong.

"If it shit back there you need to clean it up," Tony says as he heads up the stairs of the trailer.

Her puppy cradled in her right arm, Sunni closes the trunk and follows Tony into the trailer. She cuddles and kisses the puppy as she closes the trailer door. "Thought he was dead," she says.

"Could have been, damn mutt made a meal of the shower curtain," he says as he puts the beer into the fridge minus one. "Right before he crawled out of that hole your trailer got over there."

"Not my trailer no more," Sunni says.

"That's the truth, old man putting your stuff out tomorrow. Figure we can get over there later tonight and clear some of your stuff out...some of your mom's too for when she come back." He has no faith that the girl's mother will return; but he figures he would say it anyway. He cools his hands against the can of beer.

Sunni flops down on the couch, letting the excited puppy rest in her lap. "Don't matter, I don't got nothing no way," she says sadly.

Tony gives her a sympathetic look, he had figured she didn't have much but wanted to offer the chance to get anything she might think has value. "Lauren...," he pauses as if rethinking what he's going to say before he continues. "Well, you can wear her old clothes, think you the same size."

Sunni feels sickened by the idea of wearing the dead girl's clothes now. "That's okay...," she says, her voice little more than a whisper.

Tony cracks open his beer. "Suit yourself." He takes a gulp and settles down on the couch. Grabbing the remote he turns the television channel to sports; but his mind is preoccupied.

He still hasn't told Sunni about his meeting with the Captain. He glances at her as she scoots closer to him on the couch, the puppy finally settling down on her lap.

"You think Mrs. Danaski knows?" Tony finally asks her.

The question nauseates Sunni as she hugs her puppy closer to her stomach. She really just wants to forget about the whole thing. She looks shamefully at the floor. "I don't think so," she says, her voice slightly sad and awkward.

"We never really talked about what happened between you and the Captain...." He begins to slip into police mode wanting to interrogate her more thoroughly.

"Can we just forget about it? Please."

"I just got a few questions...."

Sunni lets out a labored sigh and looks away as she continues to pet her puppy.

"Why did he give you the ring?"

"I don't feel so good; can we talk about this later?"

"Just answer the question."

Sunni sits the puppy on the floor and watches it scurry off to explore the unfamiliar trailer. "He said we were married...," Sunni says.

Tony studies Sunni's profile searching for any sign that she's lying; but all he sees is distress.

Sunni finally looks at him. "He said nobody would believe me anyway."

Tony looks away and takes another large gulp of his beer. Now Sunni studies his profile. She has been waiting for him to show his true colors; but all she can see is that cold police mask that he rarely takes off. She slowly looks away again, focusing on the television and suddenly feeling tired. "He use to say I was a bad apple and that I needed him...to make me pure...said something about that ring helping...but," she shakes her head, "I don't feel so pure."

Tony rests his beer on his knee and turns to look at her again.

"He used to give them to all the girls," Sunni says as she rubs her bare ring finger. "So we would know each other...kind of like a club." She looks at Tony again. Their eyes meet for a moment; but Tony quickly looks at the television again, taking another huge gulp of his beer.

"Tony?"

"Yeah?"

"There really ain't nothing you can do is it?...I mean...I know how things are here...."

"You don't worry about that...the hand of justice is slow," Tony says, not sure if he even believes his own statement — not sure of what he believes anymore.

Chapter 11

Sunni stands alone at her chemistry lab table while the other kids are paired in twos for their experiments. Sunni scans the faces of her classmates as she hears the whispers and snickers which she's confident are meant for her. The teacher grabs a piece of chalk and turns his back to the class.

"Okay everyone we're going to break down the compounds of...," Mr. Bufflefield begins as he writes a chemical compound on the chalkboard.

Beads of sweat form on Sunni's brow as she pours the contents of one beaker into another. She can feel a dozen pair of eyes on her back as some students focus on her more than their own experiments. Once again Sunni's efforts at becoming invisible seem to be failing. Her unsteady hands try to place the emptied beaker back into its respective caddy; but she loses her grip. "Fuck...." She winces as the beaker hits the ground and shatters. Yep, no invisibility today. Her head bows as the hush of silence is followed by a collective chuckle.

Mr. Bufflefield turns around, training his puzzled gaze on Sunni. "There's a problem Ms. Brown?" he asks.

Sunni shakes her head.

Mr. Bufflefield's gaze shifts to the broken glass and then back to Sunni. "The broom and dustpan are in the closet," he says. But before Sunni can move, another girl is already approaching with the broom and dustpan in hand. "Got it Mr. Bubblefeet," the girl says, mispronouncing the teacher's name; her silver lip ring shining under the fluorescent lights as she gives Sunni a mischievous grin. Mr. Bufflefield bristles and the other students laugh at the butchering of his name. Under normal circumstances, Sunni might thank the girl or even share a chuckle at the undermining of authority; but she is so stunned at the unexpected act of kindness she only gives her a wide-eyed stare as the girl squats and sweeps up her mess.

"Let's take a ten minute break," Mr. Bufflefield says as he glances at the wall clock.

The room is abuzz again as the students chatter amongst themselves, grateful for the break.

Sunni squats to the lip ring girl's level and grabs the dustpan. "Let me help…," she says. The lip ring wearing girl grins again, seemingly cheerful despite the sunken and gloomy shadow her heavy dark eyeliner casts over her eyes.

"Patricia," she says and offers Sunni a handshake.

"Sunni," Sunni says as she reaches out to shake the girl's hand. Something familiar catches her eyes and she hesitates — it's a silver ring on Patricia's finger.

"You all right?" Patricia asks as Sunni suddenly stands again.

"Yeah…," Sunni responds, avoiding eye contact as Patricia also stands.

"I can take care of —," Patricia starts but is suddenly cut off by Sunni's stammering.

"No…uhm yeah…fine," Sunni says as she wipes her sweaty palms on her jeans and looks at the teacher who is reading his lesson plan. "Can I go to the restroom?" she asks Mr. Bufflefield.

The teacher nods without looking up. "Yes you can."

Sunni grabs her satchel, rushing past Patricia and out of the classroom which isn't a classroom in the proper sense of the word. In fact it is a worn down double wide trailer. After the old high school fell into disrepair due to years of neglect, the school district decided that trailers were the most economical alternative and a better alternative has yet to be considered. Sunni makes her way down a gravel path, keeping her head down as she passes various staff members. She cautiously approaches a porta-potty and looks over her shoulder for any sign that she's being watched. The coast is clear. She forgoes the porta-potty and takes off running. After reaching the far end of campus she ducks behind an unused trailer. Letting out a few breathless coughs she turns a large brick on its end and takes a seat. Deep breath in, deep breath out. Sunni closes her eyes and tries to calm her nerves. Her fantasies of making friends and having somewhat of a normal high school life doesn't seem like a remote possibility considering all the snubs she has experienced this first week of school. And then there is the ring on Patricia's finger. She wonders if Patricia knows…if the Captain knows what she told Tony. Another deep breath in, she tries to block the thought. A deep breath out, she opens her eyes and digs in her satchel. Pulling out her tiny pink ballet slippers she carefully fits one of her hands into each shoe as she tries to remember happier times. But that was so long ago.

"Don't think that's how ya' wear 'em," Jin says as he seems to appear out of nowhere. Sunni hadn't noticed him sneak around the right side of the trailer. She springs to her feet and immediately shoves her slippers back into her satchel.

"Fuck off!" she yells out at him, helplessly hoping that he will be scared off by her tough act as she rushes off in the opposite direction. But Jin follows her despite her tough demeanor.

"Now that ain't no way to treat a friend now is it?" Jin says as he tries to walk beside her.

"You ain't my fucking friend! You burned me!" Sunni speeds up her pace, her trembling hands clutching the satchel strap digging into her shoulder.

Jin quickly shakes his head. "No…it was an accident, your accident. You didn't listen," he says.

Sunni breaks into a jog and heads towards the main path figuring she'll be safer out in the open.

Jin watches her jog into the path. Seeing that she is taking a sharp right he says, "Might not want to go that way…Baine ain't forgot about his debt."

Sunni ignores him and returns to a fast paced trot once she has some distance between herself and Jin. Jin continues to follow but he doesn't close the gap. He keeps his distance. Sunni comes to the edge of a trailer, peeking around the corner she immediately notices a large group of boys quickly marching towards the porta-potties. She ducks out of sight and turns back only to find Jin still following her. The boy comes closer — not too close; but close enough to be heard.

"I know a shortcut home," Jin says, extending his hand to Sunni.

Sunni narrows her eyes and cocks her head to the side. "Why are you doing this?" she asks, trying to quickly figure out his angle, everyone has got an angle.

Jin lowers his hand and shrugs. "I like you," he says with a smile and motions for her to follow him as he begins to cut between a pair of old trailers. Sunni reluctantly follows Jin, keeping her distance at first but finally walking beside him as they make their way into an alley. Jin glances at her as they walk in silence for several minutes.

"Sorry about what happened back at the cook house," he says as he studies her face. "But you healed up real good. Was kinda' worried about ya' when we brought ya' back to ya' old man's place."

"He ain't my old man," Sunni says bluntly, although she had grown fond of Tony over the five month she'd been living with him. She suddenly stops walking and gives him a quizzical look, "And why you keep saving me?"

Sunni tries to remember what happened, the splash of acid on her face, the heavy hands on her body, it's all a blur. She vaguely remembers Jin telling her everything would be okay, or was that Tony? Yes, all a blur.

Jin raises his brow and smirks. "What? You ain't worth saving?" he asks.

"That ain't what I said," Sunni says as they resume walking through the alley.

Jin's smirk widens into a grin after a few more moments of silence fall between them. "Got some folks with an inkling you worth a bother…kinda' made me a bit curious what the fuss is about," he says.

Sunni glares at him as they emerge from the alley. "Go fuck yourself!" Sunni's response sends Jin into a fit of laughter.

"Feisty!" Jin says right before flashing lights and sirens interrupt his train of thought.

"Shit!" Sunni's sure she's going to be arrested on some trumped up charges or maybe busted for truancy. But she's only skipped the last 30 minutes of class so she had figured there wouldn't be a problem.

"Don't run," Jin orders. They hold their ground as the cop car comes to a stop and the door opens.

Out steps Tony. Sunni throws her hands up in exasperation and sighs, "Shit…."

"Get in the car," Tony orders her as he opens the backdoor. And without looking back at Jin, Sunni steps into the cruiser. Tony also ignores Jin and gets back into the driver's seat. He closes the door and yanks the car into drive.

"When you tell me you're going to be someplace, be there, no matter what," Tony demands as he speeds down the street.

Sunni just stares out the window, biting her nails and pouting. She sneaks a glance at Tony's reflection in the rearview mirror trying to read him; but she can only see anger. She returns her gaze to the road.

"And what are you doing with that guy?" Tony asks as he looks into the rearview mirror to see Sunni staring out the window. He takes his eyes off the road to look directly at her for a moment. "Hey! I'm talking to you," he yells. His attention off the road for one moment too long, he swerves slightly out of control, the tires screech and his eyes go forward again as he quickly regains control. Sunni stops biting her nails and clutches the door for dear life as Tony continues his lecture.

"You know that's Baine's friend?" he demands.

"They're not friends!" Sunni surprises herself, not sure of why she is suddenly on the defensive about Jin. Maybe because the boy keeps saving her?

"Sunni, you are not hanging out with that boy again, you understand that?" Tony says.

Sunni remains silent, returning her gaze to the road. Tony glances into the backseat again for a moment. But when he sees she is ignoring him, he abruptly yanks the car to the curb and throws it into park. He turns to her again. "Do you understand me?"

He has Sunni's full attention now. Her hand once again clutching the door, she nods, "Yeah, I understand."

Chapter 12

The trailer is quiet and dark for the most part. Only a small lamp illuminates the kitchen table where Tony pours over a scatter of photocopied pictures and official looking documents. "There is a connection, there has to be," Tony tells himself as he flips through the pages of Sunni's police file and takes a sip of his scotch. He clears his throat and digs the two silver rings out of his pocket. He can't seem to shake a nagging feeling that something is not quite as it seems in New Hope City. Not that things have ever been as they seem, at least not in the past four years, since the crash. He sits the rings on the table, balancing them over Sunni's police file photo, one ring for each eye. How could his Lauren and Sunni possibly have the same identical rings, given to them by the same person and he not know about it? And how could he have been so blind and unaware that his daughter was so close to the Captain? Disgusted with his own ignorance, he puts the rings back into his pocket and closes Sunni's file. A heavy weight of shame presses down on him as he glances down the hall towards the bedroom where Sunni sleeps. His inability to protect his own daughter from the cancer that's eating away at every part of New Hope City makes him even more determined to not waste the second chance he sees in Sunni — even if he can't get a simple word of truth out of the girl.

He glances at his watch — time for another night patrol. He quickly gathers his papers and files. And after tucking them into their hiding place he heads off to work.

***

Tony makes his way into the men's locker room, eyes straight ahead, lips sealed into a tight frown. The murmurs of the other officers reduce to a hush as they stare at Tony. He returns their blank stares with slight nods as he makes his way to his locker. He opens the locker and pulls out his civilian clothes, carefully laying them across the long bench. It's a nervous, make busy gesture. Most of the force has it in for him since he slugged Carlos and he's confident his unwillingness to play the bribery game makes him less than popular.

He lifts his gaze as the Captain steps out of the shower area with only a towel around his waist. Tony quickly shucks off his uniform and slips into his civilian clothing, while continuously shifting his gaze to the Captain who has stopped at a row of nearby lockers. Despite his efforts at remaining as inconspicuous as possible, Tony finds himself staring at the Captain's thighs willing the towel to open so that he can see if Sunni is telling the truth about the birthmark.

"Any reason why you looking at my cock, Gavilan?" the corner of Captain's lips turn downward as he glares at Tony.

Startled out of his trance, Tony's stammering is nearly drowned out by the laughter of the other officers, "Uhm…sorry I was just…I uhm…my mind was someplace else." He closes his locker door and again glances at the Captain just as he is lifting his leg to rest on the bench. An oval black patch stretches from the Captain's mid thigh to his crotch where it disappears behind the towel. Tony quickly averts his gaze and secures the lock on his locker. His mind is filled with so many thoughts, he can't focus. Maintaining his blank facial expression he quickly makes his way out of the locker room and into the open space where he sees Carlos working at his new desk in the far corner. He hasn't seen the man since their altercation. He cautiously moves towards him, wanting to ask Carlos about the birthmark, wanting to find out what he meant when he said he doesn't see things the way they actually are. He hesitates, staring at the man for a few moments from a distance before forcing his feet forward again and walking past a row of empty desks. But he only gets within a few feet of Carlos before the man speaks.

"Coming to whack me again?" Carlos asks without even turning to look at Tony.

Caught off guard by Carlo's question, Tony isn't prepared to give an answer.

"A guy got to watch his back in this station nowadays, don't know whose side folks are on," Carlos says as he turns to look at Tony.

"I'm sorry…," Tony starts to apologize but then changes course, "I haven't seen you around —"

"I'm a detective now," Carlos interrupts.

"I heard…you deserve it," Tony says, but he doesn't really believe he deserves it. Despite their long friendship, he sees him as a mediocre cop at best. He gives a wary smile and tries to think of the best way to ask Carlos about the Captain, Sunni and his daughter. He glances down at Carlos' desk and just when he's come up with the perfect way to broach the subject, he notices an open file. "You on that case now?" he asks.

"Yep…bunch of dead hookers showing up all over town," Carlos says.

"Kids…they're kids," Tony says.

"Yeah…well they were hooking and they dead now, so that make 'em dead hookers," Carlos insists. He can cope with it all better if he doesn't see them as kids.

Tony steps closer and tries to reach for the file, but Carlos stops him.

"Whatcha' you doing?" Carlos glares at Tony, offended that he has the nerve to touch his work.

"Just want to take a peek…," Tony says.

"These files are confidential…," Carlos says as he pulls the file from Tony's grasp and closes it. There is a silent, tense moment, and then Carlos adds, "I'll see you at the ceremony tomorrow?" Tony nods as Carlos gets up and places the file in a metal file cabinet.

Chapter 13

Red, white and blue balloons flank each side of the wooden stage. The Captain sits at the center, with school officials and city politicians on each side. A scatter of people sit on white lawn chairs looking up at a tall heavy set woman standing at a podium with a wooden plaque in her hands. She leans into the microphone, "I present to Captain Danaski this plaque honoring his dedication to youth in the city of New Hope for 15 years." Everyone claps, including the Captain as he makes his way to the podium and smiles at the rows of young adults he has mentored in the past. Most of the youths are boys; but there are also a few girls. Tony sits a few rows behind them and one aisle over. He studies their profiles and wonders how they were saved by the Captain while his own daughter had somehow slipped through the cracks. It makes him feel worse just thinking of those kids having futures and his daughter being dead. He studies the other faces in the crowd. Everyone dressed in their best with smiles tightly woven on their lips. At a glance the ceremony seems fancy and well endowed but up close the weathered foundation shows. The banner is frayed, the chairs are broken, the grass is worn down and balding and the surrounding buildings are falling apart, windows cracked and boarded up. Tony frowns as the Captain leans into the microphone and speaks.

"When I took up this post 15 years ago, I knew that I had a promise to keep to this city," the Captain begins to speak to the crowd. Tony leans back in his chair already beginning to let his mind wander again, trying to block out the ugly reality of New Hope's deterioration. His gaze skips over the faces in the audience again, there's the church brigade, they support the Captain in all he does; but Tony suspects it's mostly for the large donations they receive. He again glances at the handful of girls the Captain mentored. He considers them the lucky ones, mostly girls who avoided the darker sides of New Hope because they had somebody in their family looking out for them, staying on their case. He sighs, had he failed to look out for his own daughter? He closes his eyes in an effort to relax; but it doesn't work. He opens his eyes and scans the audience again, catching a glimpse of Carlos and another cop nearby. His brows raise — a good number of the force seem to be at the ceremony. He comes to his feet and leaves the ceremony as inconspicuously as possible. With most of the cops on duty at the ceremony or on patrol, he figures it's the opportune time to get a peek at the files he's been curious about.

Sunni enjoys the fairer view; about four blocks away she watches the ceremony from the window of an old red barn, its ancient paint chipping and peeling. From this distance the event looks festive, even regal in a way. And although she can't hear a word being said, she likes the beauty of the thing from afar despite the ugliness of what the ceremony represents. Jin idles next to her drinking in her features, not bothering to watch the spectacle in the distance. "Surprised they didn't make it a fucking national holiday," he says.

Sunni chuckles at Jin's comment. She knows that the people of New Hope worship Captain Danaski and they would probably make it a national holiday if they could. Her smile widens as she glances at Jin, not sure what to make of him; but glad to know at least one person in this town understands her. Shifting her gaze back to the colorful display in the distance, her smile fades again.

Sensing a shift in Sunni's mood, Jin slips his hand into hers. "But we're sticking it to 'em," he says. Skipping school is their weapon of choice.

Another small but genuine grin slips onto Sunni's lips as she holds his hand and continues to peer out the window, "You never did answer my question."

Jin's gaze never leaves Sunni. He enjoys the contrast of at her soft features with her world weary eyes, "What question is that?"

Sunni turns her attention from the window to watch him. "Why you helping me?" she asks. It's a question that's ever present in her mind. She had grown to trust Jin more over the few months she's known him; but she always wonders, why he wants to help her. It's such a rare thing, that she's not quite sure it's real.

"Am I?" Jin gives a mischievous grin.

"You said you were."

Jin shrugs. "Just trying to keep...," his voice trails off. He doesn't know why he is doing it. Maybe it's because he is suicidal? One thing is for sure; if Baine ever finds out he will probably kill him.

"What's in for you?" Sunni doesn't believe that anyone does anything just because they want to do right in the world. She believes that there is something in it for them if they are doing anything that seems good, even in the case of Tony.

Jin releases Sunni's hand and wanders over to a bale of hay. "Maybe I see something I like," he says, his back to her. He turns and looks at Sunni and grins when he sees her cheeks erupt into a bloom of red.

Sunni looks out of the window again, embarrassed that she let his comment get to her. "I ain't fucking ya' if that's what you want," she says.

Jin hisses and rolls his eyes. "That's not…I don't like ya' like that," he lies.

Sunni is shocked by his response, not sure if she should be relieved or insulted. Why wouldn't he like her like that?

Jin pushes off the bale of hay and quickly makes his way to her side again. "Look, Baine is still looking to get ya' back for Lucky," he says.

Sunni continues to stare out of the window, not at all surprised that Baine is still pursuing her. "And you're here to give me a message?" she asks.

Jin shakes his head. "Not at all…it's just…well…he ain't listening to nobody…but maybe I can get him to back off… but for right now, just stay out of sight," he warns her.

Sunni crosses her arms over her chest, focusing on the ceremony in the distance. Staying out of sight is something she would love to do; but it doesn't seem that easy.

"He's got a long memory," Jin says. "Lucky too." He gazes out of the window and into the distance; but he doesn't really focus on the ceremony.

"So what I got to do to get you to talk to him?" Sunni asks. There's always some type of strings attached, she's just waiting for him to reveal what they are. Her heart sinks a little bit as she anticipates his answer. What humiliating thing will she face next?

Jin shakes his head. "Nothing, like I said, I like ya." He adjusts his jean jacket; but a little sound catches his attention. It's barely audible; but it's there, he knows it. He slowly turns towards the barn ladder and studies it with a rigid frown.

"Something wrong?" Sunni asks. She looks at the ladder but sees nothing.

"Shhh," Jin says.

There's a creaking sound.

Sunni tightens her arms around her chest. "What's that?" she whispers, trying hard to see down the length of the ladder. Had they been followed? Was Lucky or Baine coming to take her back? She leans forward to try to get a good look but she can't see a thing.

"Who the fuck is there?" Jin yells towards the ladder and just as he steps forward Patricia's head pops up through the opening and she gives them a playful growl. She's laughing hard as Sunni exhales in relief and Jin glowers.

"Fucking scared ya' didn't I?" she cackles as she ascends the ladder and enters the barn loft.

"You didn't scare me bitch," Jin growls. "What do you want?"

"That the way you greet a guest?" Patricia grins as she makes herself at home, instinctively planting herself on Jin's favorite bale of hay.

"Patricia has science lab with me," Sunni interjects.

Jin gives her a surprised look. "You invite her here?" he asks.

Sunni shakes her head. "No...."

Patricia kicks her heels against the hay as she leans back grinning. "It's all right. Jin and I go way back," she says. "Ain't that right Jinny boy?"

Jin frowns. "You better not fucking tell anybody you saw me here," he says. He knows that Patricia has a big mouth and is used as a tool by Lucky and Baine. In some ways he's a tool too, he admits to himself; but at least he tries to push bits of his independence when he can.

"Calm down Jinny boy. I ain't planning to," Patricia says. "Besides, me and lover girl there good friends too. Hell the three of us like family just about." She glances around the barn. "Got something to drink?"

"No," Jin says curtly.

"Smoke?" Patricia asks.

"What is it that ya' want?" Jin asks. He figures he can skip the "friendly" banter. It's a known fact that he doesn't like Patricia even though they were once close, very close.

Sunni glances down at Patricia's hand again to see if the ring is still there — it is. A feeling of dread washes over her. She tenses, readying herself for a confrontation. "Lucky send you here?" she asks Patricia.

Patricia's expression grows serious. "No...," she says as she reaches into the breast pocket of her flannel shirt and pulls out a single cigarette, her last one. She lights it and takes a long drag as both Jin and Sunni watch her every movement. "I followed ya'," she says. She rolls up her sleeve and shows them a purple and black bruise on her arm. "Lucky give me that, say if I don't get the info on ya' he'll give me another to match." She puffs her cigarette again as she watches Sunni cringe at the bruise. "That's why I followed ya' and I figure ya' might help me out for not telling what I know."

"There's nothing to know," Sunni counters her offer. Some days she fears that Lucky or Baine or even the Captain will show up and just drag her off. But even in New Hope that type of brazen lawlessness would be too much for those who like to pretend it's a civilized place.

Jin motions for Sunni to remain silent. "Help you out how?" he asks. He resents being blackmailed; but he figures it's worth at least listening to what she has to say.

Patricia shrugs and takes another drag of her smoke. "Don't know, maybe ya' girlfriend can help. She do got a new cop boyfriend...," she says and gives a faux cough. "Sorry meant foster," she corrects herself and chuckles.

"Thought we was supposed to be friends," Sunni says. She rolls her eyes; maybe the entire performance with sweeping up the broken glass was just a way for Patricia to get closer. She's not really disappointed by it, just hardened.

Patricia raises her brows. "We are friends," she says. "But...I'm risking a lot just being here and not calling Lucky." She nods towards Jin. "He knows that. Got to get paid for all that added risk."

"Lucky suspect I'm hanging around with Sunni?" Jin asks. His question makes Sunni both nervous and ashamed. She hated keeping her friendship with Jin secret; but she also knows he will pay a heavy price if either Lucky or Baine finds out.

Patricia shrugs. "I told him you just easing her back into the life." She finally looks at Sunni. She lets a stream of smoke flow through her lips as she continues. "Baine's another thing all together."

"Tell me," Jin insists.

"For some reason he can't be convinced, he say you got a sweet spot for the girl," Patricia says as she continues to stare at Sunni. "So what's up? I mean...what's the cop got over our kind? He think he better than everybody or something?" she chuckles.

Jin interrupts, "Tell me what you want Patricia?" His words are slow, forceful and deliberate. He doesn't want her getting more information than she already has. Sunni remains silent, taking Jin's lead. She stares back at Patricia, not letting her gaze break, not even for a second. This makes Patricia laugh.

"Don't worry, I don't like Lucky or that Baine bastard anyway," Patricia says. "Like I said, just need a little something for all the added risk. If it was up to me, I'd put a bullet in both their heads." The thought makes her grin.

"Then why don't ya'," Sunni bursts out, surprising both Jin and Patricia.

Another burst of laughter from Patricia as she extinguishes her cigarette butt. "Not all of us got someone to play daddy to us," she says sarcastically. "Besides, foolish to bite the hand that feed ya', at least while it still feeding ya'...you don't seem to get that." She shrugs at her last comment, she really doesn't care if Sunni gets her central life philosophy or not, all she cares about is surviving. She sighs and looks at Sunni. "What I want?" she begins. "I want them kicks ya' got on for starters." Her response elicits an eye roll from Jin.

Sunni looks down at her sneakers. "Only pair I got," she says.

Patricia shrugs her shoulders. "Ain't my problem." She pulls some raggedy headphones from her breast pocket and says, "Need new headphones too."

Jin sighs and scowls, his patience quickly wearing down.

"You got any jeans my size?" Patricia asks Sunni.

Jin laughs. "What the fuck ya' do with ya' money?" he asks. He resents her, mostly her foolishness and what he sees as small-mindedness.

"I got money…don't worry about none of that, just giving my price is all," Patricia says.

Sunni looks at Patricia's ring again and is reminded of how the girl makes her money. The thought makes her feel ashamed and sorry for Patricia, although she's walked in her shoes. "How can ya' stand to let 'em touch ya'?'"

"Don't you fucking judge me!" Patricia explodes.

"I ain't judging…," Sunni says.

"Don't fucking judge me!" Patricia says again as her eyes narrow and fill with rage. "You ain't no better. You just have my shit the next time I see ya' or ya' gonna' be the one getting judged and sentenced bitch!"

Jin is fed up. He steps forward, fast and hard, grabbing Patricia's neck with both hands and squeezing, "How about I just shut your fucking mouth now right here!" Patricia tries to claw his hand away but it's no use.

Wide-eyed and shocked by Jin's blatant aggression, Sunni steps forward to stop him. "What you doing? You going to kill her!" she says as she tries to pull his hand away from Patricia's neck. She doesn't like Patricia's ways; but she's kinder than most people and that's not saying much.

Jin lets go and spits on the floor. "Take a lot more to kill this stupid bitch."

Gasping for air and coughing, Patricia glares at Jin but speaks to Sunni, "Now ya' get to see who he really is."

Sunni frowns as she asks herself if this is who Jin really is. She shakes off Patricia's comment and own thoughts. Grabbing Jin's hand, she leads him towards the stairs. "Let's go," she says. Jin follows, not giving Patricia another glance. He and Sunni make their way down the stairs of the loft and across the field leaving the barn and Patricia in the distance.

***

Tony sits at the kitchen table studying a photocopy of the confidential police file. Splayed out across the table are ten photos of dead child prostitutes. He studies their faces, many of them seem familiar, some of them not.

Comparing the 'dead hooker' files to his information on the Captain's youth program he notices that many of the girls were part of the program at some point. Everyone lauded the program as the greatest thing to come to New Hope City since the great crash. Troubled youth were funneled directly into the youth program in the hopes of reforming them — and no one complained. He looks at a photo of Patricia and Sunni;

but surprisingly enough, there's no youth program file on his daughter. He frowns. Is there a connection? Why are so many of the youth program girls ending up dead? He considers the possibility that it's just a very big coincidence; but he doesn't really believe that could be the case. He doesn't really believe in coincidences, he's always looking for the connections between events and people. The ringing of a phone interrupts his thoughts. He checks his pockets only to find his own phone silent. He comes to his feet, walks into the living room and rifles through drawers and coat pockets before realizing that that the source of the ringing is a drawer next to the couch. He opens the drawer and finds Sunni's old cell phone dried out and working again. He quickly answers it; but he decides against speaking. Instead, he listens, and for a few tense moments there is nothing but silence. A man's stern voice breaks through, "What did you tell him?..." Tony's mouth opens but he once again decides to remain silent. The stern voice continues, "You fucking talk and we will kill you." Tony tenses and waits for the man to say something else; but there's nothing but silence, the phone goes dead. Tony glances at the phone's display but the number is unknown. Tapping the phone against his chin he makes his way down the hallway towards Sunni's room. He pauses for a few seconds before opening the door and looking inside. Sunni is sound asleep with her puppy curled up at the foot of the bed. Tony watches her, and for a moment he imagines that it's his daughter Lauren lying there. A part of him wants to go over and hug Sunni, tell her everything will be fine, maybe pack their bags and head off to another town. But that's a ridiculous thought. Every town is just as worse as the next. He can handle a little threatening phone call; but what if they decide to make good on their threats? Not his problem. Sometimes he wishes he could think like that. But it seems that he has made it his problem. So tomorrow, yes tomorrow he will do what needs to be done so that Sunni will be prepared in a way that he never bothered to prepare his own daughter. He gently closes the door, making sure that he doesn't make any noise that would wake Sunni, or cause the mutt to start barking.

***

The couch, TV and coffee table are all pressed against the wall, along with the rolled up rug. And Sunni and Tony stand face-to-face in the center of the room.

"Lesson number one...don't ever let anyone get too close to you. Be aware of your surroundings," Tony says as Sunni looks defensive with her arms crossed over her chest.

"Are you listening?" Tony demands. "Cause distance is your friend...got that?"

Sunni nods. "Yeah...." She isn't sure how she is supposed to keep certain people away if she doesn't have the power to say no.

"But...what if...," Sunni starts.

"What if what?" Tony is already growing impatient.

"What if they're too close already...I mean like real close?"

Tony sighs. "Try to get away...disable..." — He demonstrates some fancy block move. — "And run away as fast as you can."

Sunni tries to imitate his moves but doesn't get it right.

"Don't worry about what I did...I'm going to show you a few easy moves...something simple," Tony says.

Sunni crosses her arms over her chest again and rolls her eyes. Seeing her frustration, Tony decides to reason with her. "Look kiddo, you want to be prepared for whatever comes your way, right?"

Sunni barely lifts her gaze and scowls instead of giving an answer.

"Right...." Tony's frustration grows, but he has an idea. "Okay, turn around."

Sunni doesn't move an inch. "Why?" she asks.

"Just do it," Tony orders her. He finds Sunni quite willful at times; but at the wrong times as far as he's concerned.

"I don't want to turn around," Sunni says. She doesn't like turning her back to anyone. But Tony doesn't intend to argue. He grabs her by the shoulders and forcibly turns her around. Sunni glances over her shoulder at him.

"Look ahead, this is important Sunni," he says.

Sunni lets out a huff and begrudgingly looks forward. "Fine," she says.

"Now, what do you do if someone comes up behind you?" Tony asks.

Sunni does her bad imitation of his fancy block move again and says, "And run."

"No, that's not right. I'm going to show you."

Sunni drops her arms to her side and fidgets with her fingers, wondering what Tony is doing behind her. She gets so nervous when people stand behind her.

Tony hooks his arm around her neck which sends Sunni into a minor panic. She knows it's only Tony; but it's still terrifying. She instinctively grabs Tony's arm and tries to pull it away from her neck; but his chokehold only gets tighter.

"Don't panic, stay calm," Tony grunts as Sunni claws at his arm, desperately trying to break free. "Come on! Get out of the hold!"

"How!" Sunni blurts out. He had gone over various moves; but she can't remember any of them.

"Just do it!" Tony is not the best teacher. "Kick, damn it!"

Sunni kicks outward, not at all logical; but she can't seem to think straight with Tony's arm hooked around her neck. She knows it's not supposed to be real but the feeling of pain on her neck is very real.

"Not that way, damn it!" Tony yells. "Kick me!"

Sunni kicks backwards; but not only does she miss her mark she ends up tightening Tony's stranglehold on her neck.

"Goddamn it!" Tony lets her go and walks towards the kitchen in frustration. Coughing, hacking and massaging her neck, Sunni glares at Tony as he grabs a bottle of scotch and pours a drink.

"This is pointless," Sunni says.

"Not pointless, it's important," Tony says before chugging down his scotch.

"Why do you care?" Sunni asks as she coughs and plops down on the couch, trying to catch her breath.

"Problem is you got no fire," Tony says as he pours himself another drink.

"What is that supposed to mean?" Sunni asks.

"You need fire to survive in this world."

"I am surviving!"

"No you just eking out an existence, Sunni."

Sunni's lips purse, she doesn't like being told she's not a survivor. She wants to know what the hell he thinks she's been doing for the past four years.

Tony gulps down his drink and sits the glass on the counter. "Get up," he says as he makes his way back into the living room.

"I'm tired."

"Nope, can't get tired. In life you can't take any breaks," Tony says. He claps his hands together. "So up."

Her arms over her chest again, Sunni continues to sulk on the couch refusing to get up.

"Come on," Tony says and gently slaps her across her head. This earns him a hateful glare. "Come on!" he says louder, hitting her across the head with more force. He wants to provoke her, tease out the fire. He knows she has it in her, even if his own daughter lacked it.

"Stop it!" Sunni tries to dodge his slaps; but Tony aims for her face.

"That's right! Show me the fire," Tony says as he slaps her across her face.

"Get off me!" Sunni tries to block his blows which are starting to sting. She lashes out, kicking him in the shin. Tony's response is fast and furious; he punches Sunni in the chest knocking the wind out of her, sending her onto her knees. She clutches her chest as Tony cracks his knuckles. "You're going to just sit there?" Tony asks her, his voice booming loud.

Sunni can feel a fury rising within her. She jumps to her feet swinging wildly, most of her blows missing their mark. Tony laughs. "Good! That's right, get mad," he says. "Cause that's what it's going to take." Sunni continues to swing wildly adding in a kick here and there, more of the blows hitting the mark. Tony sees an opening and lands a left hook under her eye, knocking Sunni onto the floor. He steps back and watches Sunni. "You got to learn to take a punch as well as give one."

***

Sunni stands in the barn loft looking out over the field as she waits for Jin. She can't help but smile as she sees him walking across the road and towards the barn. It had only been a few months since they first became friends; but it felt like forever. She turns towards the loft ladder as Jin makes his way up. Placing his tattered book bag in the corner, he frowns as he notices a red bruise circling Sunni's right eye. "What happened to your face?" he asks.

"Nothing…," Sunni says as she combs her long tresses over the right side of her face.

"Don't look like nothing," Jin says as he steps closer and brushes Sunni's hair out of her face so he can get a closer look.

"It was an accident," Sunni says.

"What type of fucking accident give you a fucking black eye?"

Sunni takes a deep breath and turns to look out the loft window again. She didn't feel up to this interrogation. "It's nothing," she says with a long sigh.

"That fucking cop did that?" Jin always worried that Tony was taking advantage of Sunni.

"It was an accident," Sunni insists.

"I'm going to —"

"Stop…" Sunni interrupts. "He's good to me."

Jin huffs at her response, the standard of good seems to lower with each day. He decides to change the subject; he isn't one to press an issue. He grabs his bag and pulls out a beer. "Could only get one," he says.

"You mean steal one?" Sunni gives a strained chuckle.

"Don't worry about it…I got enough money…," Jin counters as he cracks the beer open and hands it to her.

"Did you bring mouthwash?" she asks him.

Jin snaps his fingers. "Damn I forgot," he says with a sly grin.

"Jin, I can't go back home with my breath smelling like beer," Sunni groans a bit and takes a sip of the beer anyway. Looking out the window again, she tries to spot the trailer in the faraway distance.

Jin moves closer to her, hooking his chin on her shoulder and wrapping his arms around her waist. He presses his lips against Sunni's cheek; but she shirks away. Not wanting to take no for an answer, Jin tightens his embrace and tries to press his lips against hers.

"Off of me!" Sunni elbows him into the ribs — hard. Much of her beer splashes on her arm.

Throwing his hands up in exasperation, Jin backs away, not rubbing his ribs although they hurt like hell, "What the fuck is wrong with you? Huh? Ain't I showed you I ain't gonna' hurt ya'?" he asks. But Sunni refuses to look at him. She turns her back to him and once again glances out the window. She doesn't like the idea of being touched, not now, not like that, not by him; but how can she explain it to him or anyone? Jin tries to read her; but it's no use he never really knows what she's thinking. He shakes his head in frustration and finally asks, "Why ain't ya' never let me kiss ya'?" Sunni takes an uneasy deep breath as she balances her beer on the window ledge and shakes the liquid off her arm the best she can. She turns to face Jin again and the breeze feels cool against the beads of sweat on her back. "Is that what you want? A kiss? From a whore?" she asks.

"Is that what...that what ya' thinking?" Jin asks her as moves forward. "You think I care about that?" Jin tries to take a gentle approach moving closer now reaching out to place his hand on her hip. But

Sunni slaps his hand away.

"Fine, I ain't begging ya' if that what ya' want. I don't beg... I don't want ya' kissing me if ya' don't wanna," Jin gets closer, he doesn't like the idea of rejection at all and he wants to show her that he's in charge. With only an inch of space between them he leans forward so that their faces are nearly touching as he reaches behind her and grabs the beer off the ledge.

There is a long silence between them as Jin brings the beer to his lips and takes a sip. Sunni can smell the alcohol on his breath and see the beads of sweet on the bridge of his nose. Jin reaches around her again and places the beer back on the ledge, this time he stops and whispers into her ear, "I could force you."

Sunni snaps her gaze to meet his. "What?"

"I could force you but I ain't...."

It takes Sunni a full three seconds to comprehend what Jin is saying; but when she does, she is furious, "Then why don't you do it! Force me! Go ahead! Force me!" Sunni doesn't even try to conceal the hurt.

Jin remains nonchalant, even amused as Sunni goes ballistic. "Calm down...I ain't gonna force ya'. I could, but I wouldn't do that to you." He emphasizes the word 'you' as if there is something special about Sunni.

"Fuck you!" Sunni pushes past him and moves towards the stairs. Jin tries to grab her; but she yanks her arm away. "The fuck off me!" she says as she quickly makes her way down the stairs and out of the barn.

***

Sunni's face is still wet and red from sobbing as she enters the trailer.

Tony sits at the kitchen table waiting. He shifts his gaze to the wall clock.

"Thirty-six minutes and forty seconds. That's how long it takes for you to get home from school if you don't hit any stoplights and since you don't drive…," he pauses, giving her a moment to let that sink in, then he adds, "It's been three hours, 26 minutes, and 40, no wait 46 seconds," he throws up his hands, "Hell, I stopped counting."

Sunni takes quick, short breaths absolutely confident that she can't lie her way out of this one.

"Where have you been?" Tony demands.

"With a friend," Sunni huffs.

"With who? Where?" Tony asks. "And why the hell do you think you can go off without telling me?"

Sunni finally looks at Tony and says, "I'm sorry." She is always sorry, always apologizing for some infraction. Tony shakes off her apology. "Who were you with?" he asks. But Sunni doesn't answer, sensing that any lie would be immediately sniffed out. She lets her gaze fall to the floor as she crosses her arms over her chest.

"The school called and said you haven't been to class all week," Tony says as he comes to his feet and walks over to Sunni. Leaning in, he sniffs her. He's expecting to smell adolescent hormones but instead the scent of alcohol fills his nostrils. He considers himself a heavy drinker and sometimes he considers himself a strategic drinker; but he isn't one to advocate drinking especially for Sunni whom he sees as his responsibility, a responsibility he doesn't plan on shirking.

"You been drinking?" he asks, his tone betraying his surprise. He had laid down the rules and it seemed that Sunni was willing to follow them, especially after he agreed to take her in. Sunni takes a deep breath as she tries to slow her breathing.

"I can't go back there," she says, shaking her head as she thinks of school.

Tony motions towards the chair at the kitchen table. "Sit down."

Sunni shakes her head. "No…I don't belong here…" she says as she starts towards the door.

Tony blocks her path. "Where you going? Huh?" Sunni stops, not daring to try to cross his path. Instead, she turns around and heads towards the kitchen; but she doesn't sit. Once again Tony points to the kitchen chair again. "Sit down, I want to talk to you," he says sternly, trying hard to control his temper. It was a tone Sunni has become use to and one the she normally obeyed; but this time is different. She glares at him. "Why you even got me here?" she asks, the experience with Jin leaving her doubting Tony's intentions. She figures that everyone has an angle, so it must be the same for Tony. She cocks her head to the side, looking at his expression carefully, trying hard to read him. But as usual he isn't readable. Tony continues to point towards the chair and raises his voice, "Sit." But Sunni only stands there looking at him as he steps forward and grabs her arm. "Have a seat!" he says; but Sunni yanks her arm away.

"Why don't you just go ahead and get what you want!" she yells.

Tony points his finger in her face. "Don't fuck with me," he warns her. But Sunni is defiant as she steps closer to him; she's beginning to really believe that maybe she does have the right to say no, the right to stand up for herself, even to Tony.

"Who do you think you fooling?" she says, pressing her nose against the tips of Tony's fingers. "You're just like all the rest."

Tony narrows his eyes at her assessment. "That's what the fuck you think?"

"Yeah, that's what I think."

"You ungrateful little bitch."

"Come on," Sunni says, lowering her voice, her sly smirk concealing her sad eyes. "Now you don't think I would take nothing from ya' without paying ya' back now would ya'?" Because everything has a price, especially kindness. Her hands lift and rest at the neck of her blouse. She's tired of playing this game. She knows what he wants, it's what they all want, that's all she's worth to any of them. She unfastens the first button. And Tony watches her. After months of living with Sunni, it's not like he has never had brief thoughts of touching her, of taking advantage of her, of sleeping with her…he has had those thoughts and sometimes he hates himself because of it. He's not a perfect man. Surrounded by exploitation and corruption, he has found himself slowly becoming desensitized to it all no matter how hard he tries to do right. Sunni undoes another button, her gaze lowered, her fingers trembling and her mind a blank slate. She figures that it's better this way, to not examine things too closely. This is the way things are and the way they have always been in New Hope City — in every city. And it is probably the way it will always be.

Tony grabs her wrists and pulls her hands away from her blouse. And Sunni doesn't resist him as he pulls her closer. He presses her head against his chest and buries his face in her hair. Inhaling the scent of lemongrass shampoo, he holds her there and slides his arms around her back. This is the one thing he must get right, he tells himself as he rocks her gently, side to side, humming and then singing an old Italian lullaby.

Fa la ninna, fa la nanna

Nella braccia della mamma

Sunni's body quivers as she begins to sob quietly, her face buried in Tony's chest as he sings the sweet lullaby. Tony has always believed that even in a world of corruption, everyone makes their own choices and it is with that thought that Tony makes his.

***

The back of the van is made up like a home; drapes and clothing hang from racks affixed to the ceiling. Tony lies on a stained mattress between a tray of beers and a busty woman who plays with a loop of colorful beads hanging around her neck. She props herself up on one of her elbows and brushes her long purple painted nails against Tony's cheek.

"Was wondering where you been?" the busty woman asks as she gently caresses Tony's cheek.

"Busy," Tony says.

The busty woman starts to comb her long nails through Tony's dark brown hair. "Mmhmm...busy with that hot young thang," she says. Tony roughly grabs her wrist, squeezing hard enough to make her cry out.

"What's that supposed to mean?" he demands as he searches her face for an answer.

"Calm down sweetie...just stating what I'm seeing," she says as she tries to gently free herself from Tony's grasp.

"What exactly you seen?" he asks as he releases her with a hard yank.

"Well...you got that young girl living with you...that little whore," she rubs her wrists.

"She's a kid," he says, suddenly compelled to defend Sunni.

"Yeah...I know...but she don't act like I did when I was that age," the busty woman counters.

"Were you ever that age?" Tony retorts as he slips into his pants.

"Don't be mean...I'm a lot better...more experienced you know...," the busty woman says as gives a mischievous grin and reaches for a shirt laying on the floor.

"Get that out of your head, whatever ya' thinking it ain't what it is," he says as he snatches the shirt out of her hand and slips it over his head.

The woman retracts her hand and presses one of her long purple fingernails between her lips. "Okay...," she says as if she knows something he doesn't.

Tony notices a change in the woman's tone. "What you know about her?" he asks.

"I didn't know I came down here for questioning," the busty woman says as she busies herself with folding a stack of clothes.

Tony softens his voice, showing his kinder, gentler and more manipulative side. "It's just between us," he says. "I just want to—"

"Know what you getting yourself into?" the woman says and then sighs and reclines back on the stack of clothes, "Well...I know she worked for Lucky...that's all I know."

"You know the other girls?" Tony asks.

The busty woman shakes her head. "No, they off the street mostly. Clients come through ads and word of mouth, shit like that...they too precious to be on the street," she says sarcastically, a hint of resentment in her voice.

"You know where Lucky keeping them?"

"You know I can't tell you that Tony...fuck...you trying to get me killed?"

Tony squeezes the busty woman's bare thigh. "Come on...," he says.

"Couldn't tell you if I knew, they keep 'em on the move," she says. After thinking about it for a moment she adds, "But...maybe Dr. Whipple might got more information on it than I do."

"Who's that?"

The busty woman taps her finger against her temple. "Head doctor helping the working girls...she real pissed about the new arrangement on the street."

Tony frowns. "New arrangement?"

The busty woman nods. "Yeah...seems Lucky want 'em younger now...old models getting shelved."

Tony's frown deepens as he grabs the rest of his things. "All right," he says as he leaves a twenty dollar bill on the beer tray. "Thanks for the info." And he steps out the van.

Chapter 14

Under the dull glare of streetlights, Dr. Whipple wears a grey baseball cap and shoulder length curly hair as she hands out condoms and literature to working girls on the busy street. Tony watches the scene as he parks his cruiser, his gaze resting on Dr. Whipple. He steps out of the cruiser and the working girls scatter leaving Dr. Whipple alone with Tony. She turns to him and hisses, "Here to arrest me too? I'm trying to get these girls the help they need and what do you do...," she begins to rant; but Tony raises his hand to stop her. "I'm not here to arrest anyone," he says as he steps closer. "Heard you could tell me about...," he pauses and carefully measures his words, "...about the new arrangement on the streets." Dr. Whipple gives him a second look as if seeing him for the first time; she takes in his frown, the furrows on his brow and the badge on his chest. "I don't know nothing about that," she says and turns to leave him there.

"Wait," he calls out and starts to follow her. "Someone told me you were helping the girls out here and...," his voice trails off, already growing frustrated by her resistance to even speaking with him.

Dr. Whipple stops and turns to face him, curiosity replaces her suspicions. "What you care for officer? Don't seem no one else does."

Tony looks her in the eyes. "Cause uhm, it's my job," he says. That's the easy answer, if not completely a truthful one.

The woman shakes her head in disbelief and grins, she knows he has some alternative motive; but she decides to indulge him anyway. "What you heard so far?" she asks.

"Heard the new model on the street is kid sized," Tony carefully offers.

Mrs. Whipple frowns. "What else?"

Tony shrugs. "That's why I'm here," he says. "I got a kid," he pauses and for a moment considers mentioning his daughter and asking if Dr. Whipple knew her. He so much wants answers; but he's not sure if he's ready for the truth so he redirects his comments. "I'm looking after a girl...I think she... I think she was involved in Lucky's operation."

Dr. Whipple lets out a gentle sigh feeling saddened by that revelation, "Can't even get to the girls...using ads now...so they not even on the street where I can see 'em," she says as she continues towards her vehicle. She reaches for the car door.

"Wait…,"Tony says as he presses his hand against the car door, eliciting a surprised glare from Dr. Whipple. He immediately removes his hand allowing her to open her car door. "I want to help…," he says as he watches her step into the vehicle, "…help take these guys down," he continues.

Dr. Whipple smirks as she starts the car. "Well you'll have to actually get on the case now won't you," she says. She knows all about the case, or at least as much as they let her know. "I been calling the detective about those dead girls for weeks and…nothing…it's like they got it sitting on a shelf somewhere."

"What you mean?" Tony asks as he peers at her through the car window.

"What I mean is that nothing has been done…girls just keep showing up dead every week. I even offered to help…they told me to stay out of it, threatened to even arrest me, said I was endangering the girls by giving them condoms and booklets speaking out against the sex trade." She puts the car into drive and starts to pull off.

"Wait," Tony says again as he bangs the roof of the car, once again eliciting one of Dr. Whipple's indignant glares; but she stops the car. "Maybe I can help you get the information you need…there a way I can get in touch with you?" Tony asks. Dr. Whipple digs into her purse pulling out a business card. She hands it to him. "Just don't waste my time," she says and she pulls off without another word.

***

Hoping to find Carlos, Tony makes his way into the police station basement. He stops at the file room door and quietly peeks in. Carlos sits hunched over piles of papers as he vigorously writes in several files. He scratches out several key names, dates and facts and replaces them with new information; but Tony can't see what he's doing. Carlos stops suddenly and lifts his head.

"Sneaking around now?" Carlos asks.

"Sorry about that," Tony says as he steps into the file room. He tries to get a look at the papers on Carlos' desk; but his view is blocked when Carlos turns to face Tony.

"Can I help you with something?" Carlos asks in a curt and cold tone.

Tony loops his thumbs around his duty belt. "Looking to get some information on these dead kids that keep showing up around town," he says.

Carlos smirks at Tony. "Checking up on my work now?" he asks.

Tony shakes his head. "Not like that at all it's just that…," his voice trails off. He considers telling him about the threatening phone call but decides against it. "Just wondering how the case is going, that's all."

"I'm handling it," Carlos says gruffly.

Tony nods and presses for more information, "Good…got any leads?"

"Nope, nothing…may be suicides," Carlos says.

Tony's brows rise. "Suicide?" he asks. "So the girls just fucking strangled themselves?" And stabbed themselves and shot themselves and did whatever other sick and twisted thing that ultimately sent them to their graves.

"It happens," Carlos says seriously.

Tony lets out a sigh and looks away, staring at the rows of file cabinets that line the wall. He hates that his relationship with Carlos has grown distant, and distant is an understatement.

"Anything else?" Carlos asks.

Tony turns to look at him again. "Yeah…you think I can take a look at the files?" Tony asks. It's worth a shot, not that he expects Carlos to acquiesce.

"You got a lot of fucking nerve," Carlos says as he glares at Tony.

"Look, I just heard something on the street and wanted to take a look at the files," Tony says; but he has the feeling that there's something more between them than a punch and a few harsh words.

"You hear something on the street, you bring it to me," Carlos says, his voice cold, firm and strangely confident. "This is my case."

Tony glances down at the paperwork but nods in agreement. "Okay…got it," he says. But just as he's about to leave Carlos speaks up again.

"Look," Carlos starts, his voice taking on a tone reminiscent of the days when he and Tony were close friends. "I don't know what's been going on with you lately; but…it's not a good idea to butt around in this one, Tony."

Tony narrows his eyes. "What's that supposed to mean?"

"I need to explain?" Carlos asks.

Tony takes on a defensive stance. "Yeah, why don't you try it."

Carlos sighs, Tony has always been a tough nut, never wanting to really listen to anyone else and that's aggravating; but most importantly, it's dangerous. "You forget where you are, Tony? Who's in charge here?"

Tony hasn't forgotten. How could he? Everyone knows that the Captain is the king of New Hope City and that the police force is his royal court. He takes a deep uneasy breath, but remains slightly cocky. Carlos is — was a friend; but he has always viewed the man as slightly below himself. "You got something you wanting to tell me?" he asks.

Carlos rises out of his chair slowly and menacingly. "Chief don't want anyone upsetting the balance of things on the street," he says.

Tony frowns. "What the hell is that supposed to mean?"

"What, you got a comprehension problem now, Tony? The Captain wants to handle things…his way."

Tony studies Carlos' face and replays his words in his mind. So, it's true, there is a cover-up in New Hope and the Captain is handling it 'his way,' whatever that really means. Tony backs away, slowly moving towards the door, his hardened gaze never leaving Carlos. "So…you're one of them now," he says, realizing that Carlos has decided to give in and play the games of the city's police force. Just another pawn on a grand chest board.

Carlos smirks. "You were always so self-righteous," he says as Tony turns and steps out of the door.

Chapter 15

The science lab is busy with kids working through another chemical experiment. Sunni works with her lab partner, a timid girl that no one else wants to work with. Patricia approaches the pair. "Beat it," she says to the timid girl who immediately leaves the table. Patricia strikes a pose. "How I look?" she asks as she kicks out her right foot, showing off her "new" sneakers. Sunni's gaze travels down to the sneakers and she frowns as she says, "They look good on you I guess." She keeps her head lowered.

"Ya' guess? You don't sound so sure," Patricia says. "Maybe I should get ya' to get a new pair for me."

Sunni freezes, she doesn't have any money for a new pair of sneakers. She's already forced to wear Lauren's old pair which are a half size too small. She lifts her gaze and forces herself to look Patricia in the eye. "You didn't say nothing about me having to be all buddy with ya'," Sunni says. "So...if ya' don't mind, I want to finish this up." Patricia raises her brows; this is a new Sunni, someone willing to speak up for herself. She kind of likes that...respects it. But she doesn't oblige Sunni's request. She slips onto the stool next to Sunni and makes herself comfortable at the lab table just as Mr. Bufflefield begins writing on the board and lecturing. Sunni turns away from Patricia; every interaction with her is more exasperating than the one before. But for some reason, she can't quite make herself hate the girl. She's been in her shoes — and in some ways she still is. She starts taking notes, intermittently looking at the blackboard, trying her best to ignore Patricia's presence in the hope that the girl will just back off. But she doesn't. The door to the classroom trailer swings open and everyone turns to look, including Sunni. But there's no one there. Maybe it's just the wind. One of the students seated closest to the door gets up to close it; but when he reaches for the handle Baine and a member of his crew step in the threshold. The boy scrambles back to his seat and Baine and his sidekick step into the classroom trailer. Standing only a few inches from the classroom trailer door, Baine scans the room looking for Sunni. She's easy enough to find seated on the other side of the trailer, the wall on her left side and Patricia on the other. Sunni stares back at Baine, her trembling hand clutching her pen.

Baine slams the classroom trailer door closed, startling the students and Mr. Bufflefield. But Mr. Bufflefield never turns away from the blackboard, only watching Baine out of the corner of his eye. This isn't his fight; he doesn't plan to make it his fight. Baine motions for his sidekick to guard the door, and he smiles as he makes his way towards Sunni.

Sunni's hand trembles even more as Baine gets closer. "You fucking bitch," she whispers to Patricia. "You lied." But Patricia didn't lie. "He doesn't know," Patricia says so low she's not even sure if Sunni hears her; but she's confident that Baine doesn't and that's important. She has always been one to keep her deals; but this deal only meant that she wasn't to reveal the truth about Jin and Sunni — if they wanted more, they should have told her, she reasons. Baine makes a few final steps towards Sunni, stopping when he's only at the edge of the lab table. Still smiling, he stares down at Sunni whose entire arm is now shaking. She's terrified of Baine and she hates that. She wants to be brave like how Tony is trying to make her. But she's not sure she can be that person, at least not with people like Baine.

"Been hiding from me?" Baine asks, basking in the attention of the other students who are now more curious than scared. They know about Baine and his crew's reputation for brutality and they're more than eager to see a live demonstration of it. Sunni's trembling hand clutches the pen tighter and she lowers her head, her chin trying to burrow into her chest. It's an automatic response to Baine, a response she also hates. Her eyes get watery as she prepares herself mentally for the violence she's sure is next.

Baine leans against Sunni's table. "Never knew you was the book learning type," he says. He shoves her textbook onto the floor. Sunni flinches, his every move sending a wave of terror over her. She sits her pen on the desk, her shaking hand causing it to make a clacking sound against the wood. Baine shakes his head at her gesture. "Whatcha' doing? You gonna' need that to write Lucky's number down cause you must of forgot it," he says. "That's why we ain't heard from ya, right?" Without even a moment of hesitation, Sunni's shaky hand picks up the pen again. Patricia crosses her arms over her chest and frowns a little as she watches Sunni tremble. She doesn't really care much for Sunni; but a part of her sometimes feels sorry for the girl. And then there are other times that she imagines that they could be close, or that they are actually close — a kind of best friend. Baine licks his lips and squints at Sunni, "A matter of fact, I think Lucky likes it when old friends just drop by...he ain't much of a phone person...know what I mean?"

Sunni looks up at Mr. Bufflefield hoping that he will do something to help her; but he doesn't. He starts to write on the blackboard again; but he says nothing. Suddenly, Baine grabs Sunni's wrist, an action that sends a bolt of adrenaline through the girl. She pulls away from Baine; but she's unable to free herself.

"Don't fight it," Patricia advises. She knows that Baine is just looking for a reason to hurt the girl — don't give him a reason.

Baine tightens his grip. Sunni looks around for help again; but there is none. "Come on, it won't be so bad," Patricia says, her voice as calm as she can make it. "He just wants to talk." Sunni's gaze flicks from one person to the next, but she doesn't see a friendly face in the room and she also sees no other way out. She stops pulling away and resigns herself to the fact that she can't get herself out of this situation. "Okay," she says. "I just need to get my stuff." Baine releases her, allowing her to gather her things and the trio and Baine's crew member leave the classroom trailer.

***

A black SUV speeds down an alleyway, its wheels crushing the litter in the road. Inside, Baine and Lucky sit in the backseat, each guarding a door while Sunni and Patricia sit between them. There's no way out and Sunni knows it. She stares at the floor trying hard to not imagine her fate and she cringes as Lucky swings his arm around her shoulders.

"Feels like old times," Lucky says with a grin. He glances out the window and spots an abandoned shopping mall. "Right there," he tells the driver. He motions towards the shopping mall's dilapidated underground parking ramp. "Down there, that's private enough."

The driver goes down the ramp and comes to a stop at the far end of the lot. He puts the car into park and hops out of the vehicle. He opens Lucky's door, but Lucky doesn't get out. Instead, he grabs Sunni by the cheeks and forces her to look at him. His heavy fingers press hard against her gum line and the pain is so great that it takes a lot of willpower for Sunni to not cry out. His voice is just as rough and heavy as his hands, "When you coming home, Sunni?" It's not just a question, it's a demand and Sunni knows that there's no right way to answer it. She knows that as far as Lucky is concerned she can give no right answer because she doesn't own her own life. She is his property, no matter where she is. She lowers her gaze and her body is seized by a low level tremble, the fear is starting to take over. A fear that everyone can smell, especially Lucky. He releases her cheeks and Sunni feels an internal sigh of relief. At least she has a few moments more before she suffers his fury.

Lucky steps out of the SUV and motions for Sunni to do the same. "Get of the car," he says. Sunni's legs wobble as she steps out of the vehicle and tries to keep her distance. "You too," Lucky says to Patricia who immediately complies. But when Baine and the other teen boy try to step out, Lucky stops them. "You two stay there." He closes the door and forces Sunni against a nearby wall while Patricia stands a few feet away. Sunni is shaking terribly and her shoulder blades ache from all the tension while Patricia is relatively calm and even confident as she watches Lucky reach into his jacket and pull out a silver handgun. Sunni slumps against the wall and her lips quiver at the sight of the weapon. It's confirmation of her worse nightmares. He had promised her a swift execution if she ever betrayed him and she has done just that. Lucky stands several feet from the girl, the gun held at his side, its barrel pointed at the ground.

"I've been trying to be patient, Sunni," he says. "But I don't know what's taking you so long to get back home. It's not like that cop can do nothing about it. So, that makes me think you ain't really wanting to come home." He pats the gun against his thigh. "Baine say you feeling better than what you are, better than all of us. But I just want to hear it from you. What you say, Sunni? You feeling like you better than me?"

Sunni quickly shakes her head, "No."

"I didn't think so," Lucky says. "I mean cause that don't make no sense, now do it?"

Patricia's expression darkens as Lucky cocks his handgun. She initially thought he was just using the gun to scare Sunni; but now she's not so sure.

Sunni presses her back and sweaty palms against the wall. "I just wanted to...," she pauses and carefully measures her next words. What she really wants is a normal life; but she doesn't dare tell him that. To say that would suggest that he's somehow abnormal. "I just wanted to go to school," she says, her voice cracking with each word.

"That don't stop you from working," Lucky says. "Lots go to school and work at the same time." He motions the gun towards Patricia, "Look at her, she does it. Make good money too." Sunni glances at Patricia and for the first time since she stepped into the SUV she feels rage, seething anger at Patricia for helping them and sadness at the fact that the girl is just as powerless as she is.

Lucky motions for Sunni to come to him. "Let's go home," he says. "I'll take you shopping, get you some new kicks and get you back to work again. Hell, you can even go to school." He grins at her, but his eyes are fierce. Sunni knows that look. She's learned to read it and she doesn't like what it says. Life with Lucky has never been good and she knows the drill — he can easily make up and make nice; but at the same time make her suffer. Her gaze drifts to the ground. This is it; this is where she needs to take a stand. Will she let him use her and make her feel like less than dirt again? Or, is she willing to face death? Every muscle in her legs wants to give out but she struggles to stay on her feet. She won't go to Lucky, she won't move an inch. No, she has no intention of returning to Lucky's line of work, not now, not ever.

Lucky cocks his head to the side and taps his gun against his thigh again. He has never seen Sunni stand up to him — or anyone before. He steps forward, stopping only inches from the girl. He places his gun under her chin and lifts her head. "I'm a fair man," he says. "So I'm giving you a choice." He reaches into his jacket pocket and pulls out a pair of dice.

"Doubles, you can leave here alive and make your own choice about what you want," Lucky says. "If it ain't doubles, I blow your fucking brains out."

Sunni shutters her eyes and swallows hard. She had seen those dice roll a cruel fate to many people and she often wondered if they were loaded.

Lucky removes the gun from Sunni's chin and steps back, leaving a few feet between them. "Don't worry, I won't blow out all of your brains," he says. "Just the bits that ain't useful." Lucky shakes the dice as Patricia steps closer, the sharp clacking sound causing Sunni's heart to pound hard. The dice are thrown down and they hit the fractured concrete, tumbling towards Patricia's feet. She and Lucky squat to see the numbers; but Sunni is too petrified to move, she can only watch them.

"Snake eyes!" Patricia squeals, delighted that at last fortune has smiled on someone in what always seems like a stilted game of chance. But Lucky just smirks as if he knows something she doesn't. A full smile crosses his lips as he stands and looks Sunni in the eye. "Guess it's your lucky day," he says. "Your lucky day; but it ain't hers," he points the gun at Patricia and pulls the trigger twice. Two bullets strike her in the head. And the force of the impact sends her crashing face first into the ground. Sunni's mouth opens wide and for a few moments no sound comes out as she watches a stream of blood pour out of Patricia's forehead. And then there are screams — high pitched, terrible screams. Baine jumps out of the SUV, shocked that Lucky gunned down Patricia.

"What you do that for?" he asks. "Get back inside," Lucky snaps before turning to Sunni again. "All choices got consequences," he yells over Sunni's screams. Putting his gun away, he quickly moves towards the vehicle where Baine is still standing. "Inside!" he snaps again, Sunni's shrieks nearly drowning out his words. Baine doesn't argue this time; he quickly jumps into the backseat while Lucky makes his way to the passenger side. Once Lucky is settled inside the SUV, the driver revs up the engine, its sound the only noise that overpowers Sunni's wails. As the vehicle drives out of the underground parking lot, Sunni's legs finally give way and she collapses to her knees, her gaze fixed on Patricia's lifeless body. It isn't the first time that she has seen death; but it is in her mind, the first time that she has caused it. Her screams turn into sobs as she presses her hands against the ground and begins to crawl towards Patricia. Maybe she's still alive, maybe she can be saved, she tells herself. The warm blood soaks through her jeans as she kneels before the girl and lifts her head. "Patricia?" she whimpers. But Patricia's body is limp and lifeless, there's no way she could be alive, no way to save her.

***

Sunni steps through the trailer's front door. Her clothes soaked in blood, she trembles as she stares blankly at Tony sitting at the kitchen table bent over a stack of files and papers. He doesn't look up.

"What you doing home early? What did I tell you...," his voice trails off as he looks up and sees the bloody mess. He immediately jumps out of his seat. "Tell me where you're hurt, show me!" he says as he rushes towards the girl. But Sunni doesn't show him anything; she simply lifts her bloodied hands and stares at them.

"I need to get clean," she says, taking a step towards the bathroom; but Tony scoops her into his arms and leads her towards the couch. "What happened to you?" His voice is panicky as he gently sits her on the couch and frantically checks her body for wounds. He can feel his heart pounding as he carefully checks the places with the most amount of blood. And no matter how hard he tries only the worse thoughts come to his mind. "Just tell me where you're hurt," he says, trying hard to seem composed and in control.

Still in shock, Sunni continues to stare at her bloody hands. "I'm not...," she says, but her voice trails off. She slumps back on the couch. She's not hurt, not in the ways he's expecting.

"Who did this to you?" Tony asks and a dozen different scenarios run through his mind. But when Sunni offers no answer a feeling of terror rises within him. "What the hell is going on?" he asks and he can hear a tremor in his own voice.

Sunni turns towards Tony with a sad, apologetic look in her eyes. "You can't do nothing about this, Tony. Nobody can. I got to go back," she says.

"What?"

"I got to go back to him. It ain't no choice to it. I just got to."

Tony clutches her shoulders and fixes his gaze onto hers, "Whose blood is this?"

She lets her gaze remain locked onto his as she answers. "He shot her. Just shot her," she says. Her lips begin to quiver and her eyes pool with tears. "It was almost me...it was supposed to be me," she sobs.

Tony's eyes widen in disbelief. "Shot who? Who shot who, Sunni?" He doesn't comfort her. He's all business now, thinking of calling for backup, thinking of calling it in.

Sunni's chest heaves with each sob. "I can't stay here." She tries to pry herself free from Tony's grasp; but Tony tightens his grip.

"I need you to tell me who got shot and who shot them," he says firmly.

Sunni tries once again to pull away. "It doesn't matter, she's dead!" she says. "And I'm dead too if I don't go back."

Tony keeps a firm hold of Sunni, "Listen to me, calm down...." He puts on his proverbial cop hat, "Where's the body?"

"I don't know," she shakes her head as she whimpers. "I can't...."

"Yes, you can...You know who? Who did it?"

"It doesn't matter."

"It does matter!"

Tony's harsh tone makes Sunni sob harder. "I can't do this anymore," she cries out. "I don't know why I thought I could...I have to go back."

"Back to who?" he asks as if he doesn't know the answer, but he does know it.

Sunni tries to stifle her sobs long enough to answer. "Lucky," she mumbles.

Her answer deflates Tony, but he tries to keep his composure. "Lucky kill somebody?" he asks.

"You can't do nothing about that," Sunni sobs.

"Tell me who Lucky killed."

"Patricia," Sunni says.

Tony looks confused, "Who is that?"

"My classmate."

Tony's heart sinks as he slowly releases Sunni. She was just a kid, another dead kid. It's Lucky who's been killing these kids? But he's not entirely surprised.

Sunni heaves a few more sobs. "He killed her...and if I don't come back, I'm gonna' end up just like Patricia...dead," she says as she remembers Lucky's last words — choices got consequences. "I don't got no choice, Tony. Nobody can do nothing about him."

Tony rubs his face in frustration. Lucky is protected by every thug and dirty cop in the city. He punches the air at the thought. Coming to his feet quickly, he makes his way to a kitchen drawer where he pulls out his gun. He reaches under the sink and grabs a bottle of scotch. "Stay here," he orders Sunni as he marches across the kitchen and living room and steps out of the trailer, the door slamming shut in his wake.

***

Tony drives erratically through the streets. At every stoplight he lifts the bottle of scotch to his lips and takes a large gulp. He doesn't turn on his cruiser's sirens, but he does dominate the road, ignoring everyone and everything outside of his goal. He takes a hard left turn down a dirt road.

He hates that road only because of where it leads. After driving a quarter of a mile, the road stops at the expansive front yard of a large wood frame house. The sun is beginning to set and its bright illumination nearly blinds Tony as he stumbles drunkenly out of the vehicle. "Lucky! Get your fucking ass out here!" he says and then he waits and watches, but there is no stirring in the house, not that he can see. He reaches back into cruiser and snatches his gun from the passenger seat. He points it, aiming at some blurry point on the house and shoots. The bullet shatters a window. "Fucking show your face!" The veins on his neck strain as he shouts. He once again waits, looking at each window for any sign of life; but there is none. And if there is, it's well hidden. He finishes off the bottle of scotch and slumps against the cruiser, suddenly feeling impotent. "Your times coming unlucky...I promise you that, it's coming soon," he says. Tony throws the empty bottle and it smashes into the side of the house. With great difficulty, he stumbles back to the driver's side of his police cruiser and gets it. And he gives the house one last hateful glare before he drives away.

***

Sunni hides in her bedroom with her puppy sleeping on her lap. The soft mattress under her buttocks gives way slightly as she leans her back against the wall and stares into the darkness of the room. It's after ten o'clock; but it's impossible for her to get any rest with the loud sound of Tony's drunken yelling and shadow boxing coming from the living room. She reaches under her pillow and grabs a silver ring — Patricia's silver ring. And she wonders what she could have done differently. What can she do now? Is there no way to make it right other than returning to Lucky? Maybe she had it all wrong before. Maybe she doesn't really have any right...or any power to live a normal life.

She frowns at the thought, so much wanting to cry again. But she refuses to shed another tear. Not today. How many more days, weeks...hours, does she have before more consequences come about because of her choices?

There's a gentle rapping on her window, she freezes, only turning her head to see a silhouette of someone on the other side of the glass. Is it Lucky? Or, is it one of his thugs coming to teach her a final lesson? Her heart pounds hard as she imagines the worse.

"Sunni?" Jin's voice is barely audible, but Sunni instantly recognizes it. She pushes her puppy off of her lap and rushes to the window, quickly opening it. "Shhh, he's still awake," she says. She listens for the sound of Tony's voice and when she still hears his yelling she climbs out of the window, careful to avoid making any noise. Jin brushes her hair out of her face, his warm fingers against her skin giving the feeling of security she's always craving.

"Sorry I didn't get here faster," Jin says as he checks her face for any signs of abuse. "But I got over here as soon as I found out about it." At finding her face intact he gently brushes his thumb against her cheek. "What the fuck happened today?"

Sunni nearly breaks her promise to herself not to cry when she starts to think of what did happen, but she keeps her composure. "I don't know...he just shot her, rolled the dice and shot her." She slides down the wall of the trailer and sits on a plastic crate while Jin squats next to her. And for a brief moment she becomes paranoid wondering if Jin is to be her executioner.

"You okay?" Jin asks, seeing the look of terror on her face. Sunni turns to look at him and finds only the kind Jin she first met, not the sometimes cruel Jin she had come to know and even care for. "Yeah...I guess I'm okay," she lies. She knows she's never going to be okay. Things are different. She's made them different through her choices.

Jin rests his hand on her leg. It's good to touch Sunni, good to feel her next to him again. When he was first told of the shooting, the story was twisted and somehow in the version that first got to him, Sunni was dead. He'll never forget how he felt in those moments before someone offered the correct version of events.

"I don't wanna' go back," Sunni says. But she feels like she has to. Nevertheless, she looks at Jin and asks, "You want me to go back?"

"No." There's no hesitation in Jin's answer. He's sure that he doesn't want her back in the life. "You my girl. I don't want ya' part of that."

Sunni looks relieved but also troubled. Choices have consequences, consequences she doesn't want to experience. "We can leave then...," she says.

"What ya' mean?"

"We can runaway."

Jin laughs, "And go where, Sunni?"

"I don't know. It don't matter. Away from here."

Jin shakes his head, "Nah, can't leave here with no money, no nothing."

"He's gonna' kill me, you know that right?"

"Not gonna' happen."

"Yes, it is."

"Nah, he won't do that. Trust me. Don't worry. I got things under control. I already talked to him."

Sunni furrows her brow, "He listens to you now?"

"Mmmhmm."

"Why's that?"

Jin doesn't answer. He scoots closer to her and kisses her leg.

Sunni presses for answer. "Why would Lucky listen to you?"

There's a long stretch of silence as Jin thinks of a way of telling her without telling the whole truth. Finally coming up with a solution he proudly says, "Cause I'm working for myself now."

Sunni pulls away from his touch, "What you mean working for yourself?...Forcing girls cause ya' can?" She comes to her feet, disgusted before he can even answer her questions. Is he working girls just like Lucky now? Or, is he cooking meth again? Whatever it is, Sunni doesn't like the feel of it. She starts to climb back into the window; but Jin stops her.

"Hey, it ain't like that," he says as he tugs her away from the window.

"Then what is it?" Sunni demands, she wants to feel that security again, but all she feels is dread.

"I put a lot on the line for you, Sunni. And I didn't do that cause I could force ya. I did it cause I like ya', like my girl. You different. I like that." He pulls Sunni closer, interlacing his fingers through hers. "Don't you know that?" he asks. He lifts her hand to his lips and kisses it. "I plan on keeping you safe."

Sunni wants someone to look after her and keep her safe, but she takes Jin's comment with a large dose of skepticism. Bright headlights wash over the trailer and they crouch under the window. "You need to go," Sunni says as she tries but fails to indentify the visitor. She turns to watch as Jin stands and backs away. "Keep a low profile," he tells her and then he takes off across the park. She watches him for a few moments before he disappears behind a rundown, empty trailer. "You too," Sunni murmurs to herself.

She's still not one-hundred percent sure of what Jin is up to; but she's got a feeling that nothing good will come of it. Once the headlights dim, Sunni balances herself on the milk crate and climbs back into the window. Her puppy is patting at her legs as she gently steps into the room. She creeps across the floor towards the bedroom door an cracks open the door. Peering down the hallway and into the kitchen, she watches Tony step across her line of sight and disappear into the living room. She hears the front door open. And she can just barely make out a woman's voice.

"You said it was an emergency?" the woman asks with a hint of skepticism in her tone.

"You want something to drink?" Tony offers as he crosses Sunni's line of sight again, entering the kitchen with the woman only a few feet behind him.

Sunni's eyes widen when she recognizes the woman as Dr. Whipple, the psychologist who has a reputation of always looking out for the street girls. She's never met the woman personally; but she knows that Lucky hates even the mention of the doctor's name.

"I think I'll pass," Dr. Whipple says as she sits her oversized red leather purse on the table.

Tony pours himself another glass of scotch and motions for Dr. Whipple to sit.

"I can't stay for long," Dr. Whipple says, not bothering to take a seat.

Tony nods and quickly downs his scotch. Sitting his empty glass on the table, he steadies his gaze and looks into the woman's dark brown eyes. There's something intense there, something fiery despite the woman's reserved demeanor. "I know who's killing these girls," he says.

Dr. Whipple's muscles tense as she locks onto Tony's stare and she doesn't let go. "Oh?"

"Yes, that's why I called you here," Tony says as he motions towards the chair again. "Please, sit down."

Dr. Whipple tries to relax her muscles as she takes a seat, but it's not so easy. She's spent months trying to track down the killer, but it always seemed that the police were trying to hinder her — so she's not so trusting, not even of someone like Tony. "So why haven't you arrested him?" she asks.

Tony pushes his glass and bottle of scotch over so that they are directly in front of him. He pours himself another drink. It's a good way to stall so he can figure out exactly what he should and shouldn't say. Tony has his own trust issues.

After nearly ten years on the police force he's seen his fair share of shysters and losers. Even many who seem to want to help have their own agenda so he's learned to step carefully through the landmine that is New Hope City. "It's complicated," he says.

Dr. Whipple hisses at his response. It's complicated my ass is what she really wants to say; but she's much too polite for such a crass statement. "If you're not going to do anything, then why did you call me here?" she asks.

Tony traces his finger over the rim of his glass as he looks into Dr. Whipple's intense brown eyes. "I want to know if I can trust you," he says.

Dr. Whipple scoffs at his assertion — what nerve of him. Her spine lengthens and it's as if a tiny spark within her has become inflamed. "That's for me to ask you, Officer Gavilan. I'm not the one working with a corrupt police force that won't even arrest a child killer. Or, are you really going to argue that point?"

Tony puckers his lips as he continues to study her. He knows the corruption is endemic; but he likes to sometimes pretend that things are different. "You can't mention this to anyone," he says. "Not yet." At this point he doesn't know who he can trust on the force and he doesn't want to provoke the wrong people.

"Okay, that's fair enough," Dr. Whipple says, her muscles finally relaxing.

Tony taps his finger on the edge of his glass of scotch. "It's Lucky," he says bluntly.

Dr. Whipple doesn't look even slightly surprised. "Well I could have told you that. It's not a secret that he's rough on the goods," she says. "But you got proof?"

Sunni strains hard to listen closely for Tony's answer. Her hands begin to tremble, it's the prelude to a wave of fear that she's come to know intimately. Is Tony going to tell Dr. Whipple what she knows? Her heart pounds at the thought of it. She doesn't want to be involved in ratting Lucky out, but she does want him punished. It's just that rats pay the steepest price for turning informant. If she's known as a rat, she'll be dead for sure — she's sure of it. She tries to open the door a little wider to get a better look but it creaks loudly. "Fuck," she curses to herself. She tries to gently close the door, but because she's in such a rush she slams it shut instead.

Tony snaps his gaze to his right, looking down the hallway and towards the bedroom door, frowning hard as he stares at it.

"What was that?" Dr. Whipple asks as she leans forward to get a glimpse of what Tony is seeing.

"Nothing, just the wind," Tony says as he continues to stare at the door for a few moments longer. He turns to Dr. Whipple. "No, I don't have proof. There's just a rumor going around," he says, not wanting to let on that Sunni may know the details. "But I know that he killed a kid."

"Again? Recently?" Dr. Whipple asks.

"Yes."

"Do...does anyone else know about this?"

"No," Tony says quickly.

"Who is it?" Dr. Whipple asks, a weary look flooding her gaze. She's tired of hearing about the death of so many young girls whom she couldn't save.

"A kid from New Hope High," Tony says. "Patricia."

"P-p-Patricia?" Dr. Whipple stutters, her demeanor quickly growing sullen.

"Did you know her?" Tony asks.

"Yes...I did...I...," Dr. Whipple's words trail off as she runs her hand over her large, red leather purse. She keeps little necessitates and treats for the girls in there — sanitary napkins, deodorant, bars of soap and a stash of their favorite sweets. As for the girls she's lost, she keeps a small photograph of them so that she never forgets. "She was one of my girls...until she went back."

Tony stops tapping his glass. "I'm sorry...to hear that," he says.

"Yes…me too," Dr. Whipple says as she pulls her hand from her purse and straightens up. It's part of the price she pays for caring, she tells herself. She stiffens her back and forces herself to look at Tony. "What are you going to do about it…this death?" she asks.

Tony downs his scotch with two large gulps and pushes the glass to the side. "Well, I have some ideas, but like I said I don't have proof yet."

"Maybe your girl has proof," Dr. Whipple says.

Tony raises his brows, "Who?"

"Your girl…the girl you're watching."

Tony pauses for a moment, for some reason he expects that people won't notice that he's taken in Sunni, "No, she doesn't. It's just a rumor."

"But you believe it?"

"Yeah."

Dr. Whipple lets out a long, heavy sigh. "Is this why you called me here, Officer Gavilan? To tell me about rumors? Rumors we can't do anything about."

"No, I called you so I could help you."

Dr. Whipple scoffs, "Help me do what? Take the corrupt police force down? You know that's not possible, no one can do that. Or, you want my help putting Lucky in jail? You said yourself that's complicated. And we both know what that really means. No one can touch Lucky; he's got the entire force under his thumb and a lot of the so-called good people too." She stops her rant and shakes her head in frustration. "Look, I appreciate what you've done for the one girl you took in. That's more than what most do in this town, but…."

"You don't want my help?"

"It's not that."

"What is it?"

"It's just that…I don't think there's much you can do, Officer Gavilan. I'm not so sure there's a way of getting this guy behind bars, not in this town."

"What if we got a different kind of justice?"

The intensity in Dr. Whipple's brown eyes returns. "What are you saying?" she asks.

"Sometimes you've got to take matters into your own hands."

"You're talking about street justice?" Dr. Whipple's voice rises, louder than ever and certainly indignant.

"You could call it that," Tony says, not flinching and not backing down.

"All you cops really are the same, aren't you?" Dr. Whipple pushes back from the table and comes to her feet. But as she reaches for her purse Tony grabs her arm. "Don't be a hypocrite," he says.

Dr. Whipple yanks her arm out of his grasp. "Hypocrite?"

"You said yourself, there's no getting justice in this town," Tony says. "What if…we got our own justice? We could stop Lucky and the Captain and save those girls you say you care about."

Dr. Whipple narrows her eyes at Tony, resenting his suggestion that she may not care as much as she says she does. "And how would WE do that?" she asks.

"With other people, just like us," Tony says.

"Like us? Or, like you?"

"I don't think there's a difference."

Dr. Whipple shakes her head and loops the strap of her purse over her shoulder. "Street justice…sounds like you're going to make more trouble for these girls than they already have." She points at Tony, "Don't you do that Officer Gavilan, don't you dare do that."

Tony stands tall with his arms crossed over his chest as he peers into Dr. Whipple's fiery eyes. "I think I've done pretty good, so far. I've kept Sunni safe, I don't plan on changing that."

Dr. Whipple continues to shake her head, "Whatever you think you're doing…just keep my girls out of it." She turns from him and heads towards the front door.

"We'll be meeting soon, me and the others," Tony says.

Dr. Whipple pauses at the trailer's door.

"We're meeting to discuss what can be done. I'll let you know when and where," Tony says. "You can make your final judgment from that."

Dr. Whipple listens, but says nothing as she opens the door and walks out of the trailer.

Sunni continues to listen carefully, her ear still pressed against the bedroom door. But when she hears footsteps moving towards her she jumps back in her bed and pretends to be asleep.

Tony starts to knock on the door but decides against it. Instead, he roughly pushes it open. Sunni flinches as the door hits the wall; but she still continues lay there, pretending to be asleep. Her attempt at deception causes Tony to frown hard as he leans against the door frame watching her from a distance.

"You eavesdropping on me?" Tony asks, his voice loud enough to send the dog into a barking frenzy.

Sunni starts to stir as if she is just being awoken, "Huh?" She stretches and yawns in an exaggerated fashion.

Tony shakes his head in disgust. "Were you listening in on what I was saying?"

"No," Sunni says with a loud yawn.

"Get up!"

"What?"

"I said get up!"

"What did I do?"

"You lying to me that's what you did!"

Sunni sits up in the bed and shakes her head, "No, I'm not…"

Tony pushes off the door frame and slowly walks towards her. He hates liars even more than snoops. "What did I tell you about lying?" he asks as he towers over the girl, close enough that Sunni can smell the alcohol on his breath and see the veins in his neck.

"That you don't like my lies," she says.

"And…," he presses her for more.

"That if I keep lying, there's gonna' be a big price to pay."

He squats next to the bed so that he's eye level with Sunni. "So let's try it again," he says.

Sunni drops her gaze, unable to look at him.

"Were you eavesdropping on me?" Tony asks.

Sunni nods, her head barely moving; but it does move — up and down, slowly. Tony straightens up his long muscular frame towering over the girl again. He closes his eyes and massages the bridge of his nose. He isn't so sure he wants Sunni involved or even knowing about his plan; but he does need one bit of information. "Where's Patricia's body?"

Sunni leans her back against the wall and bundles her puppy into her lap. "What you gonna' do, Tony?" She doesn't want to go back to the parking lot, but even more than that, she doesn't want Tony to get himself killed.

Tony opens his eyes again. Looking down at Sunni he tries to speak calmly, "I need to you to help me."

Chapter 16

Standing before her bedroom mirror, Sunni changes out of her black dress and into a pair of jeans and a short sleeved t-shirt. She's just come home from Patricia's memorial service which was surprisingly well-attended. She fastens a thin metal chain around her neck with Patricia's silver ring looped around it. And she wonders if her own death will be noticed and mourned by much of anyone.

"Sunni?" Tony calls out from the other side of the closed bedroom door.

"Yeah?" Sunni answers as she runs her finger along the ridges of her metal necklace.

"I want to show you something," Tony says.

"Just a minute," Sunni says as she tucks her necklace into her t-shirt and opens the door.

Tony's serious expression hasn't changed much since the memorial service. It's not as if Sunni expected him to cry or anything, but she was expecting some type of emotion, even anger would do. "Put your shoes on, we're going for a ride," Tony says.

Sunni quickly slips on her sneakers and they head out of the trailer.

Both Tony and Sunni are unusually quiet as they drive down the main highway of New Hope City. They park on the shoulder and set off down the road by foot. The loneliness of the highway is a rarity, especially for an early Saturday evening. And only a few cars pass them even as their trek reaches the one mile point. "Where we going exactly?" Sunni asks as she works hard to keep up with Tony's quick pace.

"It's not far," Tony says. He points to a patch of trees a quarter of a mile away, "Just through there."

Sunni glimpses the distance of the trees and stops walking. It takes a few moments for Tony to realize she's no longer by his side. He stops and turns towards her. "What are you doing?"

"I'm tired. I need to rest," Sunni says as she bends over and presses her palms against her knees.

Tony marches back towards her. "Not here," says. "Can't have anyone spot us standing here." He grabs her arm and pulls her off the shoulder of the road and into a grassy area. "It's not too much farther," he insists. They walk through the tall grass and eventually reach the edge of the woods where they enter the thick, low lying brush just as the sun is setting. The old, towering oaks take on an ominous feel as Tony and Sunni carefully make their way through the woods. It seems that they're alone, but Sunni can't shake the feeling that someone is watching her. She snaps her head to the left and to the right; but she sees nothing. Not even a deer or a wild boar which she imagined lived in the woods. She quickens her pace and starts to ask more questions; but Tony motions for her to be quiet just as they reach a small clearing.

There's a rustling noise — several. Sunni once again snaps her head from left to right; but this time she spots three people emerging from the brush — two men and a woman. The man farthest from her right, a large, muscular man wearing army fatigues is Danny, an ex-marine with more than his fair share of war stories. The other man, wearing a dingy grey baseball cap and grungy jeans is Bobby and his past is just as soiled as his clothing. As they move closer to the trio, Sunni's gaze flicks from Bobby to Danny, neither of which she recognizes. But she does recognize Dr. Whipple who keeps her distance from the men. Danny ignores Sunni as he embraces Tony as if they're old friends. The warmth between the two men is apparent in both words and gestures; but when Tony turns to greet Bobby, he offers only a rigid handshake. Sunni tilts her foot nervously as she watches the adults greet each other. Feeling out of place she goes into her invisible mode, tilting her head down and staring at her sneakers, unsure of why Tony has brought her to the clearing. But just as she's settling into her invisible state, she once again gets the sense that someone is watching her. And as much as she wants to continue to stare at her sneakers, she feels compelled to look up — and when she does she finds Dr. Whipple unabashedly staring at her. Sunni shrinks under the attention.

"What is she doing here?" Dr. Whipple demands, her tone not angry at all, but more worried than anything. Tony presses his hand onto Sunni's shoulder blade and squeezes gently. "She knows," he says. Sunni looks surprised by Tony's comment. While she did eavesdrop on him, she's not so sure she knows what's going on at all. She starts to speak up but decides that wouldn't be a good idea. Instead, she trains her gaze on the strap of Dr. Whipple's red purse.

"What do you mean she knows?" Dr. Whipple asks as her concern grows.

"She overheard us," Tony says.

Dr. Whipple shifts her concerned gaze from Tony to Sunni and frowns. "Just great, just what we need," she says with a huff.

Danny tenses and the veins around the hairline of his military style buzz cut strain. He doesn't like the presence of the girl either. Bobby only smirks, not seeming to care one way or another.

Tony lifts his hand from Sunni's shoulder and motions for the woman to calm down. "There's nothing to worry about."

"Nothing to worry about? You know what'll happen if Lucky gets word of this?" Dr. Whipple demands.

Tony lifts his 'calming' hand again, "He won't…She…" Tony stops and glances down at Sunni, this time really seeing her and doubting if it is right to take the action he is considering. But before he can continue his thoughts, Dr. Whipple interrupts.

"What are we going to do about this situation?" she asks.

Tony takes a deep breath and looks at Dr. Whipple again, "She can help us."

"What do you mean help us?" Dr. Whipple asks.

Sunni looks up at Tony with fear in her eyes. She doesn't know what he means by help; but it's making her nervous. As if he can sense Sunni's trepidation, Tony gives the girl's shoulder another squeeze.

"Help us get close enough," he says.

"You didn't say anything about using a kid," Dr. Whipple protests.

Tony shakes his head, "She's the only one with access to what we need."

"Who we need?" Dr. Whipple corrects him.

"Yeah," Tony says.

Dr. Whipple shakes her head in disagreement, "I'm not liking this. Not at all."

"Look, we don't have much choice in the matter. It's our best shot."

Bobby wipes his hands on his grungy jeans and finally speaks up, "He's got a good point Deborah."

Dr. Whipple scowls at Bobby, "Dr. Whipple to you," she says.

Bobby raises his hand to his forehead and gives a mocking salute, "Yes ma'am."

Dr. Whipple's frown deepens as she puts her attention on Sunni and notices that the girl is trembling. "Officer Gavilan," she says. "Can I have a word…in private."

Dr. Whipple and Tony step to the side, out of earshot of the others. "I don't know what you got going on in that head of yours; but I don't like using kids in grown folks' business," Dr. Whipple says. In fact, she had only agreed to come to the meeting because she was concerned that Tony would make things a lot worse for her girls.

"She won't get hurt," Tony promises.

"How do you know that?"

Tony huffs and hesitates; he doesn't really know for sure, it's just a gut feeling or at least a hopeful one. "They're after her; she's already involved and there's nothing either of us can do to stop what's already started," he says.

"They're after all the girls," Dr. Whipple says. "Should I bring all of them down here too?"

"Look, I know you don't like this. But Lucky is coming after her and that's that. Now, if we play our cards right…maybe we can use that against him."

Dr. Whipple rolls her eyes, "How exactly you plan on doing that?" Her words drip with snarky disbelief.

Tony doesn't look at Dr. Whipple, in a way he feels guilty. Using Sunni to get Lucky hadn't been part of his original plan; but after looking at all of his options, he feels that she's the best chance they have. He finally locks his gaze onto Dr. Whipple, "I want to send her back to him."

"What?!"

"Wait, let me explain."

"Are you out of your mind?!"

Tony sighs, quickly growing annoyed with her, "It's the only way."

"No. I won't be involved in this." Dr. Whipple turns to walk away; but Tony catches her by the elbow.

"You giving up already?"

"It's my job to get these girls off the street. Not to deliver them right into the hands of Lucky."

"Yeah? Well how's that going for ya'? You said it yourself…he's got the girls on lockdown. Now we got a chance to get inside. You going to walk away from that?"

Mrs. Whipple looks at Sunni and admits to herself that it hasn't gone too well. She failed Patricia and has failed to make any headway on the teen prostitute murders. Looking Tony in the eye she says, "It's not as simple as you think, Tony. These girls…they're attached to their pimps. Even after…." She lets her gaze drift to Sunni who is waiting impatiently, just out of earshot, "Even after someone like you takes up for them. They still go back. How do you know she won't go back and stay? Rat us out too. Anything is possible."

Tony hadn't considered that. He knows that the girls can be quite attached to their exploiters; but for some reason he hadn't considered Sunni to be that type. Now there's a lot at stake. He has to be sure that she won't turn on them. He breaks away from his conversation with Dr. Whipple and makes his way to Sunni's side. Sunni straightens up as Tony rests his hand on her shoulder. "Everything okay?" she asks as they begin to walk away from Dr. Whipple and the two men.

Tony squeezes her shoulder and frowns, "I got a bit of bad news." He can feel her shoulders tense under his palm. "We're taking you back to Lucky," he says. Sunni stops walking and turns to face Tony. Is this some type of joke? It has to be some type of joke, Sunni tells herself. She gives him a half grin, half grimace as she chuckles, "What?" She shakes her head as if willing him to say he's just got a dark sense of humor and that he would never send her back, but he doesn't say that.

"I'm sorry," he says, his voice so low that only Sunni can hear him. "But he's on his way here now."

Sunni gasps and a feeling of suffocation nearly overwhelms her, making her dizzy and unbalanced. She searches out Dr. Whipple who is watching a distance away. Does she know about this? She can't possibly know what Tony is about to do, she tells herself. Dr. Whipple's face scrunches at the distressed expression on Sunni's face. She takes a step forward, but one look from Tony stops her, it says — 'let me handle this my way.' But Dr. Whipple isn't so sure she should let him handle it, nevertheless she doesn't intervene. Tony digs into his pants pocket and pulls out his phone. He taps a few buttons and reads something before slipping it back into his pocket. "Let's go," he says as he tries to guide Sunni towards the path leading out of the clearing.

Sunni glances at Dr. Whipple again, half expecting her to come to her rescue; but when she doesn't Sunni pulls away from Tony.

"I don't believe you," she says. "This some type of sick joke?"

"Do I look like I'm joking?!" Tony's rage seems genuine, so real that it startles the others. "I can't have you fucking up things! You're going back to him! You got that?!" Tony grabs her arm again; but Sunni tries to pull away.

"Please...I'll do anything!" she pleads.

Tony tightens his grip and grabs her other arm. Shaking her slightly, "What you gonna' do Sunni?"

"Anything...."

"What?" He gives her another hard shake, "Say it!"

"I...I don't know why you're doing this...."

Dr. Whipple steps forward, "That's enough!"

"Shut up!" Tony growls at Dr. Whipple, a response that stuns her and leaves her momentarily speechless. Now everyone believes. There's no doubt in their minds that Tony intends to send Sunni back to Lucky and that Lucky is in fact on his way.

Tony tries to lift Sunni over his shoulder; but she fights fiercely. Kicking and screaming she tries hard to free herself from Tony's grasp.

"Somebody help...," Sunni belts out right before Tony clamps his hand over her mouth and wrestles her to the ground.

Dr. Whipple looks to the other men for help; but they offer none. "You're sick!" she yells at Tony just as he is finally able to restrain the girl.

His hand over Sunni's mouth and his knee in the small of her back, Tony looks up at Dr. Whipple. "I'm sick?" he asks. "Cause I want to send one girl back?... If we don't get Lucky, a lot more girls like her will end up in his operation." He finally removes his hand from Sunni's mouth and a torrent of sobs escapes her lips. He lifts his knee from her back and crouches beside her. "You are going back to Lucky," he says, the hard edge gone from his voice. "But not for the reasons you think."

Sunni slowly pulls herself into a sitting position, dirt and blades of grass sticking to her clothes. She dusts herself off and fixes her hatred filled gaze on Tony. If she had the power, she would punch him, make him feel the pain and fear she's feeling. She wipes the tears from her cheek with the back of her hand and glances at Dr. Whipple and the two men as they approach. "Just stay away from me," she says. She doesn't want any of them near her, her trust is at an all time low.

"You don't have to do anything you don't want," Dr. Whipple says as she kneels next to Tony.

Sunni's look of hatred and hurt mixes with confusion. "But...he said that...."

"We had to know that you wouldn't turn on us," Tony says without offering any type of apology. "When you go back, it'll be to help us take him down."

The fear begins to return as Sunni fully comprehends Tony's words. He wants her to go back to Lucky — no way, she says to herself. Destroying Lucky is something she's caught herself fantasizing about, but the reality of facing the man is terrifying. "I don't know if I can...," her voice trails off and she glances up at the other two men who give her disapproving looks.

Dr. Whipple reaches out for Sunni's hand, but the girl quickly pulls away. The fear in the teen's eyes hurts her. She never wants to be the object of that fear. "It's okay, if you don't want to," Dr. Whipple says in as calm a voice as possible.

"No, it's not okay," Tony interrupts, his words bringing a frown to Dr. Whipple's lips. "If you don't help us, Sunni, then...," he points the silver ring hanging around Sunni's neck, "She died for nothing." And his daughter too, he says to himself. Realizing the ring has come out of her shirt during the struggle with Tony, Sunni quickly tucks it back into its hiding place.

Dr. Whipple's fiery brown eyes burn hot as she stares at Tony. "Don't pressure her. It isn't her place...," she says. Her gaze softens as she looks at Sunni again. "You don't have to decide right now."

Sunni hears Dr. Whipple's words, but she doesn't feel she has got much choice in the matter.

She quickly nods an agreement before she can talk herself out of it. She's not so sure her answer is truthful, but it's the one she's giving for now just to get Tony out of her face.

Dr. Whipple can't help but feel a sinking feeling at Sunni's response. She extends her hand and Sunni takes it, letting the woman help her to her feet. And they and the men gather into a circle, perching on various stones and tree stumps. Tony stands before them. He takes a look at each person, making eye contact as if doing so will give him insight into the their true motivations. "If we're going to do this, it has to be done, no matter what," he says. "To the death?" He needs to know how far each of them is willing to go for this mission. Will they face difficulties and abandon their posts? Bobby rubs his sweaty palms on his dingy jeans and averts his gaze. Smacking his lips he doesn't respond, he just needs to get paid. He has no interest in blood oaths, especially those which require him to relinquish his life. Deborah straightens her back and locks her gaze on Tony, "If that's what it takes, then yes...to the death." She's committed to looking out for the girls. More than anything she needs to make sure Tony doesn't make things worse on the street and worse for Sunni. Danny frowns hard as he stares into the distance, his military like camouflage making him blend into the dark woods. He considers himself a man of his word, if he takes a blood oath it will be truly to the death. He looks at Tony and then Sunni, he knows about the world the girl comes from and he's been wanting to pay back the likes of Lucky for all the low down, dirty things he's done. "Yeah," he nods. "Whatever it takes man. You know I'll do that...kill, even die too."

Sunni takes a deep breath, she doesn't want to die but she does want Lucky to pay for what he did. She resumes staring at the ground and saying nothing.

All attention is on Bobby now, they all know about his criminal past...and present, all except for Sunni. "What's it going to be Bobby?" Tony demands. Bobby finally looks up at him, "Whatever man, whatever you say." Not exactly what Tony is looking for, but it will suffice.

Tony turns to Sunni, "You're going to be our eyes and ears. I need to know who they're targeting and who their inside person is at New Hope High." Sunni nods silently, she can feel the terror and doubt creeping in; but she forces a small smile anyway. "Good...," Tony says as he watches her for a moment, "You're going to do just fine." He needs to believe that. Once again Dr. Whipple questions Tony, "And what exactly are we going to do once we get Lucky?

Tony looks at her, his eyes intense and serious, "Kill him."

Dr. Whipple lowers her voice, "And the Captain? You know nothing happens without him knowing."

"He's next."

***

Sunni lingers in the lobby of the old, abandoned arcade. It's broken video game machines manned by kids pretending to score some big victory and the crumbling concession stand holds a variety of small time drugs and weaponry. She makes her way to the concession stand where a girl smokes a joint. "Wanted to get a message to Lucky," Sunni says. The concession stand girl blows a stream of sweet smelling smoke into Sunni's face, "I look like his fucking messenger girl?"

Sunni blinks the smoke from her eyes and lets out a little sigh. "Just… he's looking for me," she says.

Concession girl leans on the cracked glass counter, "Who's me?"

"Sunni."

"What's ya' message about?"

"Tell him…." Sunni stops and a thin sheet of sweat forms in her armpits

"I ain't got all day."

"Tell him…I made up my mind."

Concession girl seems annoyed, she cocks her head to the side, "That's all you want to tell him?"

Sunni suddenly feels faint; she grasps the edge of the counter.

"What the fuck is wrong with you?"

"I'm okay." Not that the concession girl was actually showing concern.

"If that's all the fuck you want, can ya' get the fuck away from here? I'm trying to make some money."

Sunni doesn't move, she opens her eyes and looks directly at the girl, "There's something else."

"Hurry the fuck up then."

"Tell him, I want to come back."

A wide grin spreads across concession girl's lips. She chuckles and takes on a cocky posture, "So you one of them, uh?" She looks Sunni over once more, "Wait right there."

Sunni's eyes widen. She's suddenly alert and the adrenaline is pumping. "He's here?" She hadn't expected that. Lucky never comes to the Arcade, at least not that she knows of. She watches the concession girl take off and disappear into a back room. And everything in Sunni tells her to run; but she doesn't, she just stays there — waiting. A few moments pass and the concession girl reappears; but someone's with her — it's Jin and he doesn't look happy.

He quickly makes his way to Sunni's side and grabs her arm. Pulling her away from the concession stand girl, he lowers his voice to an angry whisper and his brows knit together, "What do you think you're doing?"

Sunni doesn't know if she's more afraid of Jin at this point or Lucky. Her breathing becomes heavy and quick, "If I don't go back he's going to kill me." She lets out a yelp as Jin squeezes her arm.

"I told you I was gonna' protect ya' didn't I?"

"How you gonna' do that?"

"Don't worry about it. Just know that I am."

"He shot Patricia...and he's going to shoot me."

Jin looks away and notices that many of the kids in the grungy arcade are staring at him, "Mind your own fucking business!" he yells. And the kids quickly avert their gazes.

Sunni is once again stunned by the anger she sees in Jin, he's like two people, one kind and gentle and the other rough, loud and cruel. She grimaces as Jin pulls her out the door of the arcade. "Want to talk to ya', but not here," he says.

They make their way down the street and take a 'gypsy cab' back to the old barn which has become their kind of special place.

Jin gives Sunni a shove up the stairs of the barn loft and she resists the urge to let out a cry. She doesn't want to seem so easily hurt by his cruel behavior. She nestles in the corner by the loft window massaging her hurt arm as Jin paces the floor.

"He is going to kill me if I don't go back," Sunni says again as she trembles and tries to figure out some way to keep the truth from him.

Jin stops pacing and gives Sunni a stern look, "That ain't gonna' happen."

A genuine level of panic rises in Sunni's voice, "You saw what he did to Patricia!"

"Ya' still alive ain't ya'? Huh?" He narrows his eyes and moves closer, his posture does soften a bit as he reaches out to touch her long black hair. "How ya' think that is?"

Sunni looks into his dark eyes — not as kind as they use to be, but still kind enough. She has never been too sure about why anyone would help her, especially someone like Jin — a member of Baine's crew. She looks away, suddenly feeling ashamed about her deception. She wants to tell Jin about her plans — their plans; but she doesn't want to risk it and she knows how he feels about the law. He can't stand the presence of cops and he don't trust the justice system too much either.

Jin gently caresses her hair and his voice softens considerably, "I don't want ya' back in this life no more."

"What about Lucky? You gonna' tell him I ain't working no more?" Sunni doesn't want to work; but she does want to get that message to Lucky so Tony's plan can move forward.

Jin frowns, he's not as easy going with Lucky as he likes to pretend. He thinks he's got a plan but he's not too sure. He doesn't have an answer for Sunni, at least not right now.

"I didn't think so," she says and she folds her arms over her chest.

"He don't have to know."

"You plan on playing Lucky?" Fear creeps into Sunni's voice. She knows that's a dangerous game.

Jin straightens up and pulls out his cell phone. Sitting it on a bale of hay he glances down at the girl, "I'll tell him that I taught you a lesson."

Sunni furrows her brow, "He's gonna' want proof of that."

"I'll just have to show him."

Sunni slowly unfurls her arms and tenses. She knows there's a price to be paid for leaving the stable and there's no way around it. It's either coming from Jin or Lucky. She prefers Jin. "And then after that?"

"What he don't know won't hurt him."

Sunni nods quickly and closes her eyes, bracing herself for the blows. Jin frowns and squats before her, brushing her hair from her face. "You think imma' hit ya'?" he asks. Sunni flicks open her eyes, a bit surprised but also relieved that she isn't going to get beaten. Jin takes her by the hand, the kindness in his eyes present again as he leads her to the window of the loft. Looking out over the west end of the city, he pulls her close to his side. "Ya' see all that?" he asks.

"Yeah."

"I mean really see it."

"I guess."

"That's gonna' be all mine one day."

Sunni falls silent, not sure if he's serious or if he's off on one of his day dreamy head trips. She wonders how it is that Jin has so much sway with Lucky and can get away with so much, even with Baine. Her curiosity rises, "How's that gonna' happen?" she asks.

"You'll see." He turns her so that she is facing him. "But when it does happens, I want ya' with me, just how like we are now."

He gently caresses her cheek and leans in for a kiss. And she doesn't stop him, not this time. Their lips meet. It isn't the first time he has kissed her; but it is the first time he has kissed her like this. She can feel tingling in her lips. She pushes in for more allowing his hands to wander in ways she hadn't before. She's been with many men in her short life, each experience leaving her hollow and disgusted with her own body.

But something about her moments with Jin is different. From the way he touches her when he is being his gentle self, to the way that he lets his lips linger on hers. She lets her own hands drift over Jin's slight frame in places she has always avoided. She wants this. She wants to feel what it's like to be loved in the way other girls giggle about during lunch and whisper over during the boring moments when the teacher's back is turned. Her heart beats harder, her hands shake. Does he feel her fear and anxiety pressing against his chest? If he does, he doesn't give any hint of annoyance. That relaxes her and makes her feel normal. Makes it okay when their clothes slip off and their bodies become one.

Laying nude on the floor of the loft Sunni is only vaguely aware of the time passing. The warmth of Jin's embrace is enough to keep her comfortable even under the chilled summer breeze. "I have to go home now," she says as she finally turns to face Jin and look over his body one last time. She had never imagined she would enjoy it; it was like a first time. Even Jin looks more innocent laying there, his hard scowl and serious gaze relaxed, gentle and even childlike as he smiles at her. Is that love? Sunni hopes so. She comes to her feet and puts on her clothes, feeling very different from before. And she wonders, does she look different too? As she slips on her sneakers she can't stop grinning and she can see a big goofy smile on Jin's face too. She bends down and kisses him once more, letting her lips linger for a moment. "I'll see you soon?" she asks.

Jin nods, his smile never leaving and his eyes as gentle as ever, "Yeah...soon."

Grinning like a Chester cat, Sunni backs up and nearly stumbles over her own feet. She thumbs towards the loft stairs, "I ...I should probably get going."

Jin chuckles at her. "All right, see ya' later," he says. And Sunni makes her way down the stairs and out of the barn.

More spring in her step and her head is a little higher, Sunni makes her way towards the trailer park. What she shared with Jin is definitely the highlight of her summer, if not her life. And she's feeling so good that she doesn't even notice the two mile trek it takes to get home. In no time she finds herself at Tony's trailer. And she doesn't even bother to wipe the grin off her face as she walks through the door. Tony lifts his head from his paperwork which is scattered across the kitchen table and held down by a heavy bottle of scotch. He gives Sunni a curious look as she prances through the living room.

"Things went good?" he asks.

Startled by Tony's voice Sunni stops dead in her tracks. "Uhm...," she stutters.

"Did you send Lucky the message?" Tony asks.

"Uh yeah."

Tony looks her over and for a moment is worried that she may be drunk, but her clear eyes indicates that's not the case. "Good," he says, still staring at her for a few moments longer. "You okay?"

"Yeah, I'm fine," Sunni says as she tries to wipe the grin off her face.

Tony's not so sure what she's so giddy about, but he's not in the mood for twenty questions that will probably get twenty half truthful answers. "You should probably get some rest," he says. "I need to show you some stuff early tomorrow morning."

Sunni gives a muted nod in agreement. That seems enough for Tony, so he returns to his stack of papers just as Sunni heads for her bedroom.

As she steps through her bedroom door her little puppy greets her with his waging tail and bated breath. She's glad someone is just as happy as she is. She plops down on her bed and lets the puppy curl up in her lap. Stroking its long hair she once again dreams about her experience with Jin, a special moment that she doesn't plan on ever forgetting.

Three miles from the clearing in the woods and secluded on the northernmost corner of a sprawling estate, an abandoned ranch house simmers with activity. In the living room, Tony sits on the edge of a battered rustic chair while Sunni, Bobby and Danny sit on a couch across from him. He goes over his plans for the umpteenth time with his barely attentive audience. Dr. Whipple is listening from her spot by the window but she is also peering down the long driveway where a ball of dust swirls and funnels. She squints as she catches the flicker of a silver car bumper.

"Someone's coming," she says, as she waves for Sunni to hide in one of the empty rooms. Sunni quickly comes to her feet and tries to get a glimpse out the window as she moves towards one of the doors right off the living room area. She can't get a good look at the driver, but that doesn't stop her from thinking the worse. Had Lucky gotten a whiff of their plans and sent someone to squash them? Or, had he come himself to take care of the matter personally. She opens the door to an empty room and steps inside. Once Sunni is hidden, Dr. Whipple rushes to the ranch's front door and opens it just as the vehicle comes to a stop at the base of the porch. Sunni peers through a crack in the door and watches as the driver steps out of the car, his polished boots hitting the hot dusty ground and his face well concealed in the shadow of his large brimmed cowboy hat. The cowboy hat and high priced clothing rules out that he could be Lucky or a member of his crew. The well-dressed man removes his hat and presses it against his chest.

"Ma'am, I'm here to see Officer Gavilan," he says with a large dose of annoyance and superiority in his voice. Dr. Whipple shifts forward so that her entire body takes up the doorway — she has no intention of letting him through or calling on Tony. On the other hand, she does consider giving the man a short lesson in manners. But before she can give the well-dressed man a tongue lashing for what she considers unnecessarily rude behavior Tony is standing right behind her and already opening the door wider.

"About time you made it," he says to the man. "Thought for a second, you weren't gonna' keep your word." He rests his hand on Dr. Whipple's shoulder. "He's the one I mentioned earlier," he says to her.

Dr. Whipple turns her fiery gaze on the well-dressed man one last time before turning away from him and walking towards the kitchen without even a word of welcome. Manners are important, but she doesn't feel the need to be too nice to the rude and ill-bred. Tony motions for the well-dressed man to step in, hoping that there won't be a conflict with Dr. Whipple, at least not before he gets what he needs from the man.

"Did you bring what I asked for?" Tony asks the man.

Stepping inside the ranch, the well-dressed man frowns as he glances over the dusty house with peeling paint and a cracked ceiling. He pulls his arms close to his body as if he doesn't want to dirty himself by brushing up against anything. He gives Tony an inquisitive look, "What you need it for?"

"Don't mind that. Just need to know you brought it."

The well-dressed man catches a glimpse of Bobby and Danny sitting in the living room. "What's this about?" he asks Tony.

Tony walks towards the man, stopping only a few inches from his face. "This is about you returning a favor," he says. He motions to an empty chair in the living room, "Sit down." It's not an offer, it's a command. The well-dressed man takes the seat, hiking up his pants for comfort and resting his cowboy hat on his knee. Bobby taps his foot nervously as Danny rests his arms on his thighs and studies the well-dressed man. He's never seen him around before, but he seems like the type he wouldn't mind punching one or two times just to wipe that self-important look off his face.

"A friendly bunch," the well-dressed man says as he reaches into the pocket of his blazer and pulls out a bottle of pills. "You know…I can't be involved in this."

"You already are my friend," Tony says as he snatches the bottle out of the man's hand. "You already are." He reads the side of the bottle and furrows his brows; it's all Greek to him. "What's a lethal does?" he asks the man.

The well-dressed man loosens his necktie and glances at the others before answering, "Three will do it for a grown man. I suspect that's what ya' need it for."

"I said none of your fucking business," Tony says as he makes his way to the kitchen only a few feet away. He hands the bottle to Dr. Whipple and turns to face the well-dressed man again. "How much to knock a man out, but not kill him?"

The question makes Dr. Whipple pause as she unlocks a drawer and slips the bottle of pills inside.

The well-dressed man slowly shakes his head, "Just one or two…maybe…depends on how long ya' need him out for and how big the man is…."

Dr. Whipple slides the drawer closed and locks it before turning to watch Tony's response.

"About my height, a bit stockier," Tony says as he waves his hand a few inches above his brown hair.

"One pill should do it," the well-dressed man says with a shrug.

Tony nods slowly, satisfied with his answer. "Okay, then I'll call you when I need you again," he says as he makes his way to the front door.

The well-dressed man lifts his hat from his knee and stands. "I thought our business was limited to this here transaction," he says.

Tony opens the front door. "I'll let you know when our business is finished," he says, leaning against the doorknob.

The well-dressed man frowns and slides his cowboy hat back on his head. He quickly steps across the room and out the door. As soon as Tony slams the door shut, Sunni steps out of her hiding place. "Who was that?" she asks.

"None of your business," he says as he makes his way to the window and watches the well-dressed man step back into his vehicle and drive off. Sunni crosses her arms over her chest and frowns. She doesn't like the fact that she's on a 'need to know basis.' She wants to know everything. She wants to know every part of this plan in which she's participating.

Dr. Whipple slips the key into her purse sitting on the kitchen counter and walks back towards the other two men in the living room. "I don't like that he was here," she says. "The fewer people who know about us, the better."

"There's nothing to worry about from him. I've got him right where we need him," Tony says as he turns from the window. Reaching behind the couch, he grabs a navy blue duffle bag and sits it on the coffee table. "Have you heard from Lucky?" he asks Sunni.

Sunni shakes her head, "No, not yet."

Dr. Whipple looks surprised, "Nothing at all, not even a message?"

Sunni shakes her head again, "No." Feelings of guilt creep up on her as she carefully avoids mentioning her encounter with Jin.

"Strange," Dr. Whipple says as she frowns and makes her way to Sunni's side. "You sure he got the message?" she asks. Tony looks into Sunni's face to see if there is any hint of a lie.

"Yeah, I'm pretty sure," Sunni says, trying hard to keep a poker face.

"Who did you give it to?" Tony asks.

"Just like how you said…I went to the old arcade and uhm left it there."

Tony studies her face a little longer as he taps his fingers on the duffle bag again. "All right, as long as you sent the message, that'll buy us time."

Dr. Whipple wraps her arm around Sunni's shoulders, "You don't need to actually see him. You know that right?"

Sunni takes deep breath and lets out a long sigh.

Rubbing Sunni's arm Dr. Whipple says, "All we need is for you to draw him out…."

"She knows that all ready," Tony interrupts. He gives Sunni a strained smile, the stress has been building every since he decided to make his move. "Right?" he asks Sunni.

Sunni gives a quick nod, "Yeah. I know."

Tony unzips the duffle bag and pulls out a small bundle wrapped in a floral blanket. He sits the bundle on the coffee table and waves Sunni over. "Come here," he says.

Sunni slips out of Dr. Whipple's embrace and makes her way across the room. Stopping a few inches from Tony, she glances down at the bundle as he unwraps it. Her eyes widen when she sees a set of daggers — two intricately carved, metal handles protruding from leather sheaths.

"Not that you're going to need this," Tony says as he unsheathes one of the daggers. "But you can never be too safe."

Sunni shakes her head, her mouth drying out and a swirl of anxiety in the pit of her stomach, "I don't know how to...."

"It's not too hard, we're gonna' teach you," Tony says. "Once you get the hang of it, you'll be fine." He hands the dagger to Sunni, handle first. But Sunni doesn't take it.

"Go ahead, hold it," he says, pressing the dagger against Sunni's hand. She reluctantly wraps her fingers around the heavy knife, her grip tentative and weak.

Tony shakes his head and repositions her hand on the handle. "Hold it like this," he says. "Nice and tight. You don't want to lose your grip on it." Sunni tightens her grip, the rounded curves of the metal handle pressing into her palm. A sudden paranoid fear of cutting her own hand off by accident grips her. She's not sure she's ready for this, but she's also excited by the idea of being armed and prepared to defend herself. She glances at Dr. Whipple and immediately sees the disapproval in her eyes. She becomes uneasy under the scrutiny.

"If someone gets it out of your hand they can use it against you," Dr. Whipple says.

"That's why she's gonna' learn how to use it properly," Tony retorts.

"It's okay," Sunni says, starting to sit the dagger on the coffee table, but Tony stops her.

"No, it's not okay," he says. "I can't always be there. So you've got to learn to defend yourself." He takes the blade from her and sheaths it. Bundling the knives up, he tosses them back into his duffle bag. "Let's go," he says and motions for Sunni to follow him outside. He grabs the duffle bag and steps out into the hot summer sun. Sunni can feel the humid heat envelop her as she follows Tony into the yard. Dr. Whipple closes the door and watches them from the window.

Tony digs into his bag again, pulling out a plastic dagger. "There are a few ways to hold a knife," he says, pressing his thumb against the tip of the handle and keeping the dull edge of the blade facing outward. "Today I'm gonna' show you two."

Sunni steps closer and studies Tony as he flicks his wrists to position the knife in various ways.

"This is called a defensive grip," Tony says. "It's good when someone is up close on you." He pulls the blunt point of the handle to his chest and then quickly thrusts the blade outward before pulling it back. "Thrusting and slashing," he says. "Works best for this grip." He relaxes his hold on the faux dagger and hands it to Sunni. "You try."

Over the course of forty minutes, Sunni and Tony engage in knife play with the plastic dagger. He teaches her various defensive tactics which she can barely understand, let alone mimic. But Tony soldiers on, breaking each move down in to its basic parts so that she might really get what it is she needs to do.

"Don't let 'em get a hold of that arm...keep it close...be quick...keep your eyes focused...watch 'em," he says as he dramatizes offensive moves and guides her through the defensive tactics. He takes a few steps back and reaches into his bag. "I want you to practice with the real one now," he says, pulling out one of the daggers and handing it to Sunni. She takes it and removes it from its leather sheath. Feeling the weight of the heavy metal in her hands, she practices holding the knife with the two grips he taught her. Tony pulls a bottle of water from his duffle bag and sits on a nearby tree stump. He takes few swallows of the water as he watches Sunni handle the blade. "You're doing good," he says.

Sunni grins, happy for the approval. "Yeah?" she asks, not because she misunderstood him, but because she wants to hear him say it again.

"Yeah, really good. You're learning fast."

Sweat rolling down her face, Sunni pulls the blunt handle to her chest and demonstrates a few simple thrusts and slashes. "Was this your daughter's?" she asks.

Tony stops mid-swallow and purses his lips. He sits his bottle on the grass and lets the cool liquid roll down his throat before answering. "No, no they weren't."

Oblivious to Tony's discomfort, Sunni continues with her line of questioning, "She had her own then?"

Tony shakes his head, the corner of his lips turning downward. If only he had the forethought to give his daughter daggers, he wonders if it would have made a difference. He shakes his head again. "No...," he says, suddenly becoming annoyed. "Why all the questions?"

Sunni stops playing with the knife and notices Tony's serious expression. "Uhm, sorry...I...just..."

"It's all right. I'm not mad," he says, pulling some of the severity out of his face with a slight smile.

"I was just curious," Sunni says. "You don't talk about her much…I just thought, you had given her…," her voice trails off. She had never heard Tony speak of his daughter much although her image is everywhere in the little trailer they share.

Tony gives a sad smile. "No, she uhm…she would never touch a knife. Too sweet for that." He glances back towards the window spotting Dr. Whipple watching them, the look of disapproval still plastered on her face. He quickly looks away, focusing on Sunni again. "She wasn't a fighter, Sunni. Not like you."

His words surprise Sunni. She's never really considered herself a fighter — not really a fighter. She's always considered herself more of a survivor, kind of like a cockroach, just durable. But she takes Tony's words as a compliment anyway and a small smile spreads across her lips.

Tony chuckles, "Yeah. But I plan on making you a better fighter." He comes to his feet and reaches out for the dagger. Sunni returns the blade to its sheath and hands it to him. "So, is it okay for me to go now?" she asks.

"Go where?" Tony asks.

Sunni pauses for a moment before answering, "Raj asked me to help him out with some stuff at the grocery store," she says, hoping that he believes the lie. "Yeah, I wanted to earn a little extra money. It's just a one day job."

Tony looks surprised, "Raj, gave you a job?"

"Yeah," Sunni says. "He said part of the money could go to pay him back for some of the stuff that happened before…well, you know before I met you."

Tony chuckles and nods at the idea. "Well, I guess you really are learning fast," he says. "Okay. I'll have Deborah take you into town; I still have some things to take care of here."

Sunni lets out a huge sigh of relief. "Great, uhm…I guess I'll go get her then?" she thumbs towards the ranch house and heads for the front door.

***

The late afternoon sun heats up the interior of Dr. Whipple's beige sedan even with the windows rolled down. Sunni lets the strong winds whip across her face and through her long black hair as they speed down the interstate highway.

"You got many friends here, Sunni?" Dr. Whipple asks.

"Huh?"

"Friends? You know people you can hang out with that are your own age and not old folks like us?" She chuckles but she's dead serious. She reluctantly agreed to let Sunni lure Lucky into their trap, but she's not so comfortable with her missing out the best part of being a teen.

"Uhm not really…well, yeah…I guess."

"You don't sound so sure." Dr. Whipple glances at her and notices a little smile. "That could only mean one thing."

Sunni fights the urge to grin at the thought of Jin. "What's that?"

"It could only mean that it's a boyfriend. Girls are never too sure about them."

Sunni's cheeks redden. "He's not my boyfriend," she mumbles.

"I knew there was a boy involved," Dr. Whipple says as she takes an exit ramp off the highway.

Sunni turns to look at Dr. Whipple. "He's a good friend," she says. "A real good friend."

"We all need those…that's the truth."

"Do you have close friends, Dr. Whipple?" Sunni asks.

Dr. Whipple tightens her grip on the steering wheel as she stops at a red traffic light. "Not anymore," she says. "Friends are a rare thing."

"So…you use to be friends…close friends?"

The light turns green and Dr. Whipple drives forward, taking a left turn. "Mmmhmmm," she says with a little nod.

"So you're not friends with them anymore…was it because you had too many secrets?"

Dr. Whipple glances at Sunni, "What's this about Sunni? You got something you want to ask me?" She's hoping to redirect the line of questioning away from her personal life.

Sunni looks out the window again staring out at the ramshackle rows of commercial buildings lining the busy street. "Just wondering if when you love…care for someone, if you should tell them everything. Or, if you…if it's okay to keep secrets."

"Sometimes secrets are all that's keeping people together."

Sunni looks at Dr. Whipple again, "So it's okay."

"If it's a secret that'll hurt them…yeah, it's okay…some secrets it's best to keep to yourself," Dr. Whipple says as she parks in front of the grocery store.

Sunni's face brightens as she smiles at the woman. "Thanks for the ride," she says.

"Anytime," Dr. Whipple says.

As Sunni steps out of the vehicle she can feel Dr. Whipple watching her. She doesn't dare turn back, lest the woman see right through her deception. She steps through the door propped open by a black doorstopper, but she doesn't go all the way in. As soon as Dr. Whipple drives away, she turns on her heels and makes down the street in the opposite direction.

***

Sunni walks for a more than an half an hour before reaching the mostly deserted block where the abandoned arcade is located. She slowly approaches the building from the side, careful to watch for any parked or approaching cars — there are none. Spotting a large blue dumpster on the side of the building she quickly perches herself behind it and peers through the small slits in one of the arcade's boarded up windows. It's nearly 6'o clock but just as hot as ever and that's probably why the hangout is mostly empty. She spots a few girls sitting around a tabletop game and chatting. Only one of them is familiar — the clerk with whom she left her message. She looks around to see if she can spot Jin, but she doesn't. The hard pounding in her chest surprises her. She hadn't felt afraid on her way over, only determined. She had it all planned out in her mind — she would confront Jin. Well, not right away. First she would spy on him, discover his secret, the one she believes she already knows and then she would confront him...better yet, convince him that he's on the wrong side of things. She envisioned that he would be understanding and even thankful. But looking into the arcade and being confronted with the reality of what she's doing she's beginning to fall from under her own delusional spell. She takes a few deep breaths and exhales, trying to even out her breathing. And then she waits.

Jin's voice is the first thing she hears when he walks through the arcade entrance.

"What you doing over here?" Jin demands as he swiftly makes his way towards the arcade girls who abruptly stop their chatting.

Sunni smirks as the girls come to attention like little soldiers in Jin's presence. Maybe Jin's got his own army, she says to herself.

"I'm not doing nothing," the girl clerk says as she nervously rubs her arms.

"What you mean nothing?" Jin asks as his lips twist into a scowl.

"I'm just hanging out —" the girl starts to explain but Jin's hard slap across her face interrupts her. Sunni's grin fades as Jin slaps the clerk again and yells, "You don't hang out when you come up short!"

The girl presses her hand against the rising welt on her face. And Sunni turns away from the sight, but she can still hear him demanding money from the girl and demanding that she work more and get more clients. She closes her eyes. It's not exactly a surprise, more of a disappointment, to confirm her suspicions that Jin is doing more than just cooking a little meth for Lucky and being one of Baine's sidekicks. She folds her arms over her stomach trying to contain the sickly feeling of sadness threatening to push up and out of her. The talking in the background stops. She looks through the window again but doesn't see him. She looks over the top of the dumpster and sees him walking across the street and cutting through the gangway of two buildings. Quite impulsively, she decides to follow. She doesn't know why she's following, she just does. It's not as if she hasn't received her answer already — she has. But she needs something else, something more. She keeps a good distance while stalking Jin through the mostly abandoned section of the city. She's unable to keep track of the time, but it seems that more than an hour has passed once they reach the homeless encampment with its throngs of destitute citizens begging for a handout or a customer. Concealed by the frenzy of activity, Sunni picks up her pace and closes the distance with Jin, slowing down only when she's no more than a few feet behind him. The encampment's homemade shelters become a blur and the strong scent of frying meat and human excrement fill her nostrils. A rough hand digs into her arm and for the first time since she began following Jin she takes her gaze off the boy to look up at the homeless man towering over her. His back hunched and his head bowed, he extends one of his grubby hands while holding her with the other. Sunni wrests her arm from his grasp and shakes her head — she has nothing to give. Once she's a safe distance away from the man Sunni looks to get Jin in her sights again, but he's gone. She breaks into a jog, looking about frantically, hoping that she hasn't lost him for good. But once she reaches the edge of the homeless camp she spots him crossing the busy four lane street. She rushes into traffic, dodging speeding cars and just barely making her way to the safety of the median; but before she can battle her way through the rest of the heavy traffic, Jin disappears down a shadowy residential block. After a few false starts, Sunni is able to get across the final two lanes of traffic and catch a brief glimpse of Jin entering a house only three doors down from the corner. Sunni leans against a thick oak tree to catch her breath and stop the trembling in her hands. Now is the time to turn back, she tells herself. She can only imagine what's inside that house and part of her doesn't want to know for sure. But something within her pushes her to keep probing; she needs to know the whole ugly truth. She cautiously approaches the house, the shadow of the trees concealing her as the sun sets. The house looks abandoned but as she walks around the side she notices a light beaming through the security bars of a basement window. She steps closer, the missing glass allowing her to hear the hum of voices even a few feet away. She presses her back against the brick siding and squats next to the window so that she can listen while still remaining hidden. The first voice she recognizes belongs to the Captain.

"We need to keep it respectable," the Captain says. There's a hum of agreement right before Lucky's voice is as clear as ever to Sunni. Her heart races as he speaks.

"Of course Capt'n," Lucky says.

There's a loud creaking sound like a door opening, which is quickly followed by the telltale thump of someone walking down a flight of wooden stairs.

"Come on in boy," Lucky says.

"Got payments for ya'," Jin says. His voice is barely audible, but it's clear enough for Sunni to get a sick feeling in the pit of her stomach. There's no denying it now, Jin is definitely working for Lucky and it's not just drugs — it's girls. She clenches her fists as she remembers how Lucky's 'employees treated her in the past and for the first time since she first met Jin, she wonders if his kindness has all been a setup, some elaborate plan to get her back into the life. Maybe Tony is involved too, she muses as her paranoia runs wild. There's a long awkward silence in the basement conversation, and for a split second Sunni fears that someone will come rushing around the side of the house and discover her. She stiffens and shrinks, her stomach churning and a massive headache threatening to erupt in the center of her head.

"Sit it over there," Lucky says, his voice flat and a matter of fact.

"Hope ya' plan on paying taxes," the Captain says.

"Of course boss," Lucky responds quickly, not allowing the Captain any chance to continue. The level of compliance in his tone is something that shocks Sunni. She's tempted to look through the window to see if it's really the Lucky she knows, but she doesn't for fear of being seen.

"He's a good kid," the Captain says.

"Yeah, he is," Lucky says, his words slow and drawn out as if he is contemplating whether or not he should say them. "Not for hire though." He grins and the Captain lets out a loud bellowing laugh. Making a tsk tsk sound, the Captain says, "Always hard to find the good ones."

"Yep it is," Lucky says.

"We should get to business then?" the Captain asks.

There's no talking, only the scraping of a chair across concrete and the shuffling of feet before a girl's whimpers cuts through the silence. Sunni's eyes widen as she listens closer as if she might make out who the girl is just by her cries.

"She's a fresh one," the Captain says. "I figure you can tame her?"

"Come on, you know if I can't tame her, no one can," Lucky says with chuckle. "Boss, I was wondering, what you plan to do about Gavilan. Hear he's putting his nose in business that don't belong to him."

"Don't worry about that, I've got someone on it," the Captain says.

And then there's another long stretch of silence, followed by the stomping of feet on the wooden staircase. They're coming out of the house. Sunni takes off running towards the back of the house. She makes her way into the alley without being seen. She crouches behind the garage, her heart pounding and her breathing heavy as she sucks in the humid night air. She tries to listen for the men as her head spins with more questions than answers. What does he mean he has someone on it? Will the ranch be raided? Do they know that she's deceiving them? A chill runs through her body, sending up a blanket of goose bumps on her skin. She doesn't have any answers, nor does she hear any footsteps coming her way. Only the sound of a car engine lets her know she's in the clear. She pushes off the garage and quickly makes her way towards the alley's exit. It isn't safe to be in such a secluded place after dark. She tries to remain alert but her mind flints from one thought to the other, mostly thoughts of Jin and their friendship. Is it real? She crosses her arms over her stomach as the sickly feeling returns to the pit of her belly. She's got to do something about this. She can't let Jin be swallowed up by the life, even if he thinks that's for the best. It's not for the best, she tells herself as she shakes her head and finds herself at the alley exit. She looks around carefully to make sure no one is nearby before jogging back towards the busy street. She needs a moment to think, she needs to clear her head. She crosses the busy four lane street without much hassle and enters the homeless encampment.

The nightlife of the homeless encampment is lively, the cornucopia of sounds offer a blanket of white noise that allows Sunni to become lost in her own thoughts. She wanders through the encampment, blindly, her eyes seeing but not really because she is busy envisioning every horrible scenario that could play out if something doesn't change and change fast. She shuffles past the vendors selling drugs openly. Even the cops don't go into the encampment after dark and if they do it's because they're coming as customers. What a terrible place, Sunni tells herself. What a terrible person the Captain is and she blames him for much of her losses — the loss of her mother, her happiness and now the loss to Jin too if something drastic doesn't change.

New Hope views the Captain as the savior, the one to right all the wrong things and people — to straighten them out. Sunni frowns at the thought. She suspects —no, suspect is not right, in fact, she knows that the Captain knew about the cold-blooded murder of Patricia and the other girls. She imagines that maybe he joked about it, the way that he laughed in the presence of the whimpering girl in the basement. She imagines that they will kill her and Jin too once they've finished using him. Maybe they will kill everyone in town, just for fun and move on to the next place to devour. Sunni stops walking. It's because of the Captain that people like Lucky can exist and run the city, she tells herself. Suddenly her mind becomes still, just as still as her body and she realizes that only one thing can be done that will make any difference at all. Someone must kill the Captain. Yes, someone must kill him and that someone is her.

Sunni turns around and walks back towards the busy street.

She stands on the side of the road, close enough to the edge to be seen by drivers. And it isn't long before a pickup truck stops. A man with dirty blond hair and rotten teeth rolls down the passenger side and offers gritty grin.

"How much?" he asks.

"Just need a ride," Sunni says tiredly.

The man looks her over hungrily as he opens the passenger side door. "Get in, I'll give you the ride of your life," he says. Another car approaches and its headlights flood the truck. Sunni backs away and shields her eyes as she tries to get a look at the driver of the second vehicle. The truck driver pulls off and the other car, a van, pulls closer to Sunni and dims its headlights. Sunni relaxes as she makes out that the driver is a woman — a friend — well not exactly a friend; but someone she knew from the life. Sunni gives a quick smile and steps to the window. But before she can say anything the woman driver speaks up.

"Lucky got you back out on the street already, sunshine?" the woman asks, her long purple fingernails hanging over the steering wheel.

Sunni's smile fades as she shakes her head, "Not on the street. Just need a ride."

"Hmm," the busty woman says with a hint of disbelief.

"Look, I just need a ride out to the interstate," Sunni says, letting out an impatient sigh.

"Got a client out there?"

Realizing that she isn't getting anywhere fast, Sunni offers a lie, "Yeah, a client, can you give me a ride or not?"

The woman's smile returns and brightens, "That's all you had to say, sunshine," she says as she opens the passenger door. Sunni gets into the van, but before taking a seat she checks the back area of the vehicle where the woman's clothes hang on rods suspended from the ceiling. Always check the back, that's the first lesson of the street — surprises are always bad. After Sunni shuts the door, the woman lifts her long purple nails, turns the steering wheel and drives the van back onto the busy street.

The woman taps her long purple fingernails on the steering wheel as she pulls onto the interstate highway. There are only a few cars that share the road, but lots of potholes. She swerves left and then right, skillfully avoiding each craven in the road.

"That's a fine man you got there," the woman says.

Sunni snaps out of her own thoughts. "Huh?"

The woman gives her a 'you know what I mean' smile and says, "Good in bed too, ain't he?"

"Uhm, I have no idea what you're talking about," Sunni says.

"Aaah come on! Don't be ashamed, girl. It ain't like I'm gonna' steal him from ya'"

"What...," Sunni says, and then it dawns on her that the woman is talking about Tony. "It ain't like that!" she snaps.

Sunni's denial makes the woman chuckle. "Come on now. It's me you talking to, sunshine."

Sunni huffs in frustration and stares out the window. "He ain't like that, you got him all wrong."

"Do I?

"Yeah, you do."

They continue along the interstate highway in silence for a few moments before the woman asks, "Where you want me to drop you off along here?"

"Not too much further — just about a mile from exit 451."

The woman nods and asks, "You mind me asking...how much that cop paying you?"

Sunni clenches her fists. "Stop right here," she demands.

"Now come one now, you can tell me."

"Right here!" Sunni yells and then she calms down, not wanting to waste her energy warring with the woman. "Please."

The woman pulls the van onto the shoulder. Sunni jumps out and slams the door harder than she means to. But the woman doesn't drive off right away. Instead, she rolls down the passenger window, surprisingly unfazed by Sunni's outburst. "Lucky ain't gonna' like you meeting clients out here," she says.

Sunni crosses her arms over her chest and avoids eye contact. "He knows," she lies, hoping the woman doesn't take the initiative to double check the facts herself.

"Okay then, have it your way," the woman says, leaning back into her seat and driving off.

***

After a fifteen minute hike through the woods Sunni makes her way to the ranch house. Walking up the steps she's relieved to see no cars parked out front. She pulls out her key and opens the door. She's shocked to find the light on and Bobby standing in the kitchen. "Oh...hey," Sunni says, lingering in the threshold of the front door, not sure if she should proceed or turn back on her heels. Bobby certainly isn't part of her plan.

"Didn't hear you and Tony drive up," Bobby says as he walks around the counter and glances through the open door.

"Uhm...he's not here with me," Sunni crosses her arms over her chest and takes a deep breath.

"Well he ain't here," Bobby says. "So...you need something?"

While still lingering in the front doorway, Sunni unconsciously looks over at one of the kitchen drawers. Bobby follows the direction of her gaze. "You all right?" he asks.

"Yeah, I'm fine," Sunni says as she quickly steps forward. "I just needed to get something." She tries to open the kitchen drawer, but it's locked.

"Left something in there?" Bobby asks.

"Yeah, got the key?" She barely looks at him as she glances over her shoulder.

Bobby steps forward, patting his pants pockets. "Nope, but...," he pulls out a small pocket knife and flips it open. "I got this." He motions for Sunni to step to the side as he sticks the tip of the blade into the drawer's keyhole. A little fiddling on his part and the drawer opens without even a hint of trouble. Sunni reaches for the bottle of pills sitting atop a stack of receipts but Bobby beats her to it. He dangles the pills before her, "This what you looking for?"

Sunni locks her gaze on to the pills, "Yeah, thanks for your help." She reaches out to grab the bottle of pills, but Bobby pulls it just out of her reach. Sunni glares at him.

"What you need this for?" Bobby inquires.

Sunni gives a small huff, "Tony need 'em."

"Why I find that hard to believe?"

"I don't really know but, he sent me down here...."

"He sent you down here?" Bobby chuckles. "In the middle of the night?" He locks onto her gaze. "If you trying to get high on these...."

Sunni pffts at him and shakes her head, "No, it ain't like that."

"How about I just give Tony a call...," Bobby starts to pull out his phone.

"Wait!"

Bobby stops and looks at her.

"Please...," Sunni says.

"Then tell me."

Sunni takes a deep breath and slowly exhales. "I need to take care of this myself."

"Take care of what?"

"Of the Captain."

Bobby's eyebrows arch. He's genuinely surprised by that answer. He lets out a short chuckle. "Take care of him how?" he asks, but there's a small hint of anger in his voice that gets Sunni's attention.

"I don't know...," she says hesitantly. "He's the reason why things are like this...Lucky too...but... if the Captain goes Lucky goes too."

"And YOU think you can get rid of the Captain?"

Sunni takes on a defensive posture, "Yeah, I can…I can get close to him, like how Tony said."

Bobby smirks and shifts the bottle of pills in his hand. "You know I can't let you do that," he says. "Something happen to ya' and Tony would kill me."

Sunni lets out a sigh of disappointment and shifts her gaze to the door, regretting that she mentioned anything to him. "Right…well…I guess I should get going then." She turns to leave. A hateful scowl comes over Bobby's face as he watches her walk to the front door, but he quickly replaces it with a fake smile. "But…," he says.

Sunni turns to find him smiling at her.

"Maybe I can make it so you don't get hurt," he adds and turns back towards the kitchen, motioning for Sunni to join him. But she's hesitant, standing by the door and trying to figure out if he's pulling her leg.

"What do you mean?" she asks.

"What I mean is that you need an experienced hand to guide you," Bobby answers. "I'm watching my own back just as much as yours."

Sunni cautiously steps forward as Bobby pops open the bottle and fingers out a single pill. Rolling the tiny white capsule between his thumb and forefinger he speaks in a conspiratorial tone. "Don't think ya' be able to give him a pill like this…." He looks at Sunni, "But I know the Captain got a good appetite that just might serve us well."

***

Bobby drives a beat up 1985 Plymouth through the trailer park entrance. He comes to a stop one block from Tony's trailer. Sunni sits on the passenger side, balancing a foil wrapped plate of food on her lap.

"Remember, you can't speak a word of this to anyone, especially not Tony," Bobby says.

"Yeah, I got that part," Sunni says and she steps out of the vehicle, slamming the door shut behind her.

Sunni creeps up the trailer steps, balancing the plate of food on the palm of her hand. But before she can search through her pockets for her key, the door flies open. Tony stands in the doorway glaring at her, his gun tucked into the waistband of his pants.

"Where have you been?" Tony demands, his voice is curt and direct.

"At Raj—"

"Stop lying," Tony says as Sunni's puppy barks at his feet. Sunni can smell the strong scent of alcohol on Tony's breath, that's never a good sign. She starts to back up, but before she can escape Tony grabs her arm and pulls her into the trailer, nearly causing her to drop her plate. "You need to stop fucking lying!" He releases his grasp and stabs his finger into her chest. "I want to know where you been."

Sunni rebalances the plate in her hands as she backs away from Tony.

"What's that?" Tony demands as he motions towards the plate.

"It's nothing…just food."

"Food? From where?"

"Uhm…," Sunni continues to back away until she's pressed against the kitchen table.

Tony tilts his head to the side and furrows his brow as he examines her. "You been with that boy?"

Sunni's eyes widen as she fears that he may know what she's been up to. She shakes her head, "No…."

He slaps her across the face, the single blow nearly bringing Sunni to tears. Her puppy whines and runs under the couch. And with shaky hands Sunni sits the plate of food on the table next to the bottle of scotch and empty glass. "You're drunk," she says and starts to walk away. But Tony's words stop her. "I thought you were different," Tony says. "That you had changed. But you really don't give a shit about what's at stake, do you?"

"That's not true," Sunni says. "I'm doing everything you said to do."

Tony shakes his head and frowns. "Did you tell your little boyfriend about us?"

"No…."

"You protecting him? Is that what it is?"

Sunni crosses her arms over her chest and looks away. She admits to herself that she's protecting Jin, but not in the way that Tony thinks.

"So you figure, you'll just throw poor old Raj under the bus," Tony says as he reaches past Sunni and pours himself a glass of scotch. "Let him be the fall guy for your low-life boyfriend?"

Sunni inches out of his way and glances up at the scowl on his face. He catches her looking before she can turn away and stare at the linoleum. "I don't know what you're talking about," she says.

Tony presses the glass of scotch to his lips and takes a sip as he stares at Sunni's profile. "What do you think happened when I went over there to Raj's place looking for you? Huh?"

His question causes Sunni to look up again, her gaze locked on his. She had forgotten about the lie she told him earlier so she could conduct her unauthorized investigation. She starts to come up with another tall tale, but gauging Tony's level of drunkenness, she ultimately decides that remaining silent may be the best strategy.

Tony swishes around his glass of scotch. "What do you think happened when he swore up and down that he hadn't seen you?"

Sunni's eyes narrow and her nostrils flare. "You don't got no right spying on me," she says.

Tony releases his index finger from the glass and points it at Sunni. "I want you to tell me, Sunni…what do you think I did when Deborah said she was for sure that she had seen you walk in that store? Huh?"

Sunni tightens her arms around her chest and glowers. She imagines that he did nothing. What could he do? "Look, I'm sorry...I...."

Tony raises his hand to stop her. "I want you to take a guess, Sunni."

Sunni shakes her head, "I just needed some time alone and I didn't mean to —"

"Take a fucking guess!"

His anger startles Sunni. Her heart pounding, she wipes her sweaty palms on her sleeves. "I don't know," she mutters.

"You don't know? Or, you don't care?"

"No...I care," she lies. She doesn't even like Raj, so she certainly doesn't care much for him. She's mostly concerned with herself and being caught and exposed.

"I'll tell you what I did...," Tony gulps down the rest of his scotch. "I put a bullet in his head."

Sunni nearly trips over her own feet trying to get away from Tony. She presses against the kitchen counter as she stares wide-eyed at him. "What?"

Tony doesn't move, instead he pours himself another glass of scotch. "I'm not going to allow anybody to take you away from me again," he says, momentarily forgetting that he's speaking to Sunni and not his daughter Lauren. He takes a large gulp of the drink and clears his throat.

Sunni's entire body quakes as she clutches the edge of the counter, "You killed Raj?"

"Maybe."

"You're fucking crazy!" Sunni pushes off the kitchen counter and tries to rush past Tony but he catches her arm.

"What's it going to take, Sunni? Huh?" He pushes her down into the kitchen chair. "What's it going to take to get you to stop and consider what's really at stake?" He squeezes Sunni's arm and lets out a long sigh. To him it doesn't seem that Sunni will understand only words. "Stay here," he says. He lets her go and quickly walks towards the couch in the living room.

Sunni watches him, her hands trembling in her lap as Tony reaches under the couch and drags the whining puppy out by the nape of his neck. Sunni tenses as he makes his way back to her and drops the puppy in her lap. Clutching it tightly, she tries to comfort the whining canine. As she runs her fingers through the pup's soft coat and lets it lick her face, Tony's gaze softens, but only for a split second. He looks away, lest his kinder self take over and render him incapable of following through on his plans. He reaches under the kitchen table and pulls out his duffle bag. Sitting it on the counter, he avoids looking at Sunni, but he can feel her watching his every move. He unzips the bag and pulls out the bundle of daggers.

"When you tell a lie," he says and then pauses, carefully considering his next words as he sits the bundle of daggers on the table and unwraps them. "It's like you're killing truth."

Sunni stares down at the daggers as she clutches the puppy's warm body against her chest. "I'm sorry," she murmurs.

"You're always sorry, Sunni…," he says as he looks into her fearful eyes and pushes one of the daggers forward. "Pick up the knife."

Sunni looks at the knife and then at Tony, his eyes bloodshot red. And then she looks at the front door. She could make a run for it, but she doesn't think she would even make it across the living room. She starts to sit the puppy on the floor to free her hands, but Tony shakes his head. "No, keep him on your lap," he says.

Sunni glances up at Tony again and then quickly looks away. She swallows hard as she reaches across the table and wraps her fingers around the handle of the dagger. For a moment she considers charging Tony with it, not to kill him, but to injure him just enough to stop him from doing whatever thing his drunken mind is telling him. Holding the dagger in her hand, she leans back in the chair and settles her gaze somewhere just below Tony's bloodshot eyes.

"I want you know what it feels like to murder the truth," Tony says.

A flicker of confusion lights up Sunni's eyes as she lifts her gaze to meet his. "What?..."

"Kill him," Tony says.

Sunni furrows her brow, "Kill who…" and then it dawns on her. She looks down at her puppy and then back up at Tony, a sense of horror seizing her. She shakes her head and clutches her puppy tighter.

"You've got to learn…that sometimes the consequences of your actions can be so different from what you think they are…that's what you got to learn," Tony says.

"Why are you doing this?" Sunni whimpers, both anger and fear in her tone.

"Either you do it…or, I will," he says.

Tightly clutching her puppy, Sunni tries to run away, but Tony grabs her. Her puppy whines and squirms as they struggle. When she's unable to get out of Tony's grasp she tries to stab him but is easily restrained.

"You need to know what it feels like!" Tony says as he wrestles her back to the kitchen table. "Lies aren't little things; they're big…with big consequences. Now, someone has got to pay the price." He forces her back into the kitchen chair. "I'm doing this because I love you and I want you to learn that lies can sometimes hurt innocent people." He manages to get the puppy onto the table and hold it there. He can feel Sunni's tears on his arm as he positions the dagger in her hand over the dog. "Do it, now," he says.

Sunni looks up at Tony, her gazed filled with fear, hurt and anger and her hands trembling, but she doesn't comply.

"Now!" Tony demands as he forces her dagger wielding hand downward, stabbing the puppy in the stomach. Blood oozes out of the wound as the puppy whines and howls. "Finish him off, Sunni. Don't let him suffer."

Deep sobs push through Sunni's lips as the sound of the puppy's cries send her over the edge of grief. Her puppy's suffering is too much to bear. The feeling is worse than what's she had to endure in her own suffering. Is this what it feels like to hurt the innocent, to kill the truth as Tony says?

She slowly stands and pulls the dagger out of the bloody wound. For a moment she wishes she could fix her, put her back together. But even Sunni can see there's no saving her puppy. She lifts her dagger high, stopping just when it's level with her shoulder and after giving her puppy one final glance she plunges the blade into his chest.

Chapter 17

It's 8 o'clock and the hot sun is already beaming down on the trailer park. Outside of Tony's trailer Sunni stands over a mound of dirt that covers her dead puppy. She adjusts her satchel on her shoulder and walks towards the road. Her heart is heavy but she's even more determined to carry out her plan than before. She agrees with Tony about one thing, someone has got to pay the price and she believes that ultimately it should be the Captain. She adjusts the plate of food in her satchel and pats one of the side pouches to double check that her dagger is still there. She gently sighs, glad to have a little protection just in case things don't go as planned. The walk is a long one, but before she can ponder how much time has passed, she looks up to find the familiar rows of tidy houses in the better off section of New Hope. She makes her way down the various side streets until she finds herself standing across the street from the Captain's house. She had made that trek a dozen times before, sometimes watching him and his wife and kids and imagining herself as his wife. A silly and disgusting thought, one she now regrets. And it makes her feel a bit ashamed that she was so naive to the true game he was playing in the beginning. She perches behind a parked car when she notices the Captain's vehicle approach and watches as the wife and kids hop out and make their way up the concrete steps. She had watched them many times before, but her heart pounds in her chest as she weighs how she will alter their lives. She waits until they're out of sight before stepping out from behind the parked car and quickly crossing the street. The Captain swings around to face her before she can say a word. His eyes blaze hot with biting disapproval, a look that makes her feel small.

"Hey," she says nervously, crossing her arms over her chest.

"What are you doing here?" the Captain demands, his voice harsh and threatening.

Sunni glances at the house and spots Mrs. Danaski staring out the window with a frown etched on her lips. "I need to talk to you," Sunni says as the Captain also glances up at the window.

"Not here. You know you ain't never supposed to come here," the Captain says. "Now get!" He shoos her away and turns to go up the steps.

"She already knows," Sunni says as she rubs her finger across her necklace with the silver ring on it. "And she's gonna' know about Patricia and the rest too, if you don't hear what I got to say."

The Captain turns on his heels and rushes towards Sunni, getting in her face, "You watch yourself now, don't get yourself in no trouble you can't get out of." He glances down at the ring on her necklace and smirks. "Gavilan put you up to this?"

"No," Sunni says without hesitation. "This is between me and you."

The Captain chuckles and shakes his head. "Me and you?"

"Yeah."

"I'll tell ya' what, I'll talk to ya. That ain't a problem."

Sunni looks surprised. "Okay...." She had expected to be rebuffed, but his agreement to meet with her leaves her with actually following through on what is now becoming more than just some far fetched plan.

"Meet me at our place," the Captain says. "Tonight at 8 o'clock."

Sunni feels a sick feeling in the pit of her stomach — their place is the last place she wants to be. The memories associated with the low-rent hotel room leaving a scar upon her psyche. But she nods. She'll meet him there, but it will be the last time.

***

Carrying her plate of food wrapped in foil, Sunni walks up the rusty, metal steps that lead to hotel room #303. She approaches the door and lifts her fists to knock, but before she can, the Captain opens the door. Her throat clogs with fear as his wide, charming grin greets her. She swallows and tries to wash away her terror; but to no avail.

"Come on in sunshine," the Captain says as he opens the door wide and motions for her to come inside. Sunni steps through the door looking around the familiar room. It was always the same place, the same room with everything in its proper place. The Captain is a man of habit. He slowly closes the door but leaves it unlocked, an action which eases Sunni's mind. Sunni walks to the far side of the room and turns to catch him watching her as if she's some strange insect. The Captain is fascinated by small, delicate things and has an extensive collection of insects that he enjoys examining and experimenting on. And while some people fear strange looking insects, the captain finds them fascinating in a distasteful way and he sometimes takes great pleasure in breaking their tiny wings.

"So, what did ya' have to tell me?" the Captain asks.

Sunni sits the plate of food on the dresser. "Are you hungry?" she asks, stalling for time.

The Captain steps forward and lifts the foil on the plate, taking a peek inside. "My favorite?" he grins as he gets a whiff of the fried chicken and fries. "Well that's mighty kind of you sunshine."

Sunni watches as he picks up the plate of food and takes a seat on the edge of the bed. He pats the empty space beside him, but Sunni keeps her distance unconsciously touching her satchel and adjusting its position on her shoulder. The Captain smiles at her and removes the plate's foil. "A home cooked meal is always better than hotel food," he says. "Tony feeding you well out on that ranch?"

Sunni's eyes widen and her throat becomes dry as she considers the possibility that the Captain has been spying on her.

"Now you didn't think that would be kept a secret, now did you?" he says.

Sunni tries to steady her breathing as she reaches down to her satchel's side pouch.

"Not so fast," the Captain says, his voice freezing Sunni's action. "We wouldn't want to ruin a good time, now would we?" He sits his plate of food on the bed and walks over to Sunni. He lifts the satchel off her shoulder and sits it at her feet. There's a knock at the door and a tiny voice with a heavy Spanish accent. Sunni's eyes fix on the door as it opens and a woman wearing a maid's uniform steps inside.

"Oh, sorry, I not know you in here," the maid says, catching a glimpse of Sunni. "Your daughter?" she asks as she grabs the small trash can nearest the door.

The Captain smiles at the maid and brushes Sunni's hair out of her face, "No, my wife." The maid's eyes widen but then she quickly looks away, emptying the trashcan without further comment other than to say, "Very pretty," on her way back out the door. Her reaction gives the Captain a chuckle which is reduced to a smirk as he notices Sunni trembling.

"Have I ever hurt you sunshine?" he asks her. Sunni shakes her head, not daring to look at him. He had indeed hurt her, but in ways no one had warned her about. "You hungry?" the Captain asks as he scratches his face. Sunni doesn't respond, her mind preoccupied with how she will get the Captain to eat the poisoned food so that she can get free of him and Lucky.

"Here, let me help ya' out," the Captain says as the steps away and grabs the plate of food off the bed. "You made this yourself?"

Sunni swallows and nods, "Yes," her voice not more than a cracked whisper.

"What? I can't hear you sunshine. Cat got your tongue?" he steps closer and lifts a drumstick, "Oh but wait, this piece, this isn't your favorite." He looks over the food as if he is searching for something, "No wings? What? You weren't planning to dine with me?" He falls silent, letting the question linger in the space between them, a space which seems to be shrinking. Sunni's gaze drifts to the carpet, "I ate already," she says with a tremor in her voice.

"I bet you did; but you weren't selfish were you? You saved all the best pieces for me," his voice becomes lower, quieter but more intense. He steps closer, so close that his breath flutters Sunni's bangs. Sunni's trembling becomes more obvious and she hates herself for being so afraid. She wants to be strong, to shove the food into his face and make him eat it. The Captain tilts his head downward and sniffs her hair, "Strawberry," he says flatly then more gruffly, "You know I hate strawberries." He lets his hand move to her breast. Sunni pushes his hand away and tries to punch his face. "Don't touch me!" she yells, but he quickly blocks her blow. Clutching her arm, the Captain gives it a hard twist. "So you've got spunk now?" Sunni lets out a cry and struggles to get away but he's too strong. He pushes her against the wall and hooks his forearm under her chin.

"I can do whatever I want to do to you!" he says.

Sunni cries out, "Help! Somebody help!" But the Captain laughs and mocks her, "Help!" he imitates her in a whiny voice. "Help…," he draws out the word letting it teeter on his tongue. "Where could your little savior be now?" He asks rhetorically. "Officer Gavilan! Gavilan! He looks around the room as if expecting to see Tony discretely tucked in a corner. Sunni glances over to the door leading outside as she continues to struggle. The Captain follows her gaze, "What? You ready to leave already? But we've only just begun," he slams her head into the wall.

"Bobby!" the Captain calls towards the closed bathroom door. Sunni looks shocked; certainly it's a different Bobby. The bathroom door opens and out comes Bobby. Sunni is crushed, she had trusted him and he betrayed — her life seems to be a series of betrayals. Tears flow down her cheeks as she glares at Bobby. "You lied!"

Bobby only grins and shrugs, "It ain't personal kid. Just business."

***

Tony paces the floor as it gets later. He looks at the clock on the kitchen wall — it's well past midnight. Sunni has never stayed out this late. For the one hundredth time he calls Sunni's cell phone and for the hundredth time there is no answer. He cusses the phone and tries to leave a message; but there's no more room. Slamming the phone shut, he heads out of the trailer and hops into his police cruiser.

It's eerily dark and quiet in New Hope as he drives through the trailer park first and then the downtown streets in the hope of finding Sunni. But there is no sign of the teen. On his second rotation around the perimeter of downtown's main street he spots Dr. Whipple in her usual spot handing out condoms and literature to the street walkers. He keeps his distance; but tries to make his presence known while not scaring off the prostitutes. After a few moments Dr. Whipple notices him. She gives a final greeting to one of the girls and walks over to Tony's car. She leans into the passenger side window. "What are you doing here? Thought you wanted to keep this low key," she says.

"I do…look I got a problem. Sunni hasn't come home," Tony says.

Dr. Whipple looks surprised, "Did you call her?"

"Of course," Tony says.

"And?"

"And nothing. I was hoping you might've seen her or something."

Dr. Whipple shakes her head, "No, sorry, I haven't."

Tony sighs hard and looks to be at a loss for what to do. "Where is she?" he asks mostly himself.

"But…," Dr. Whipple says as she gathers her thoughts.

"But? You know something?"

"Well, I think she has a friend?"

"A friend?"

"You know…a boyfriend."

Tony sighs as he thinks of Jin. "You know where I might find them?"

Dr. Whipple shakes her head, "No, but…well, Lucky might know…well, since he's cut from the same cloth. Did you check in with him?"

Tony gives her a jerky shake of his head. "I haven't been able to get in touch with him."

"You left a message?" she asks.

"Yeah, he hasn't returned my call." He turns the ignition.

"What are you going to do?"

"Pay Bobby a little visit," Tony says as he rips out of the parking space and heads towards Bobby's apartment.

***

Tony parks his cruiser in front of the brick apartment building. He glances up at the second floor window and calls out, "Bobby!" But there's no response. He tries to open the door leading to the hallway but it's locked. Using the butt of his gun, he breaks the long rectangular window and opens the door from the other side.

He wastes no time climbing the stairs. Coming to a stop at Bobby's apartment, he starts to knock but finds that the door is open. He readies his weapon as he cautiously enters the trash strewn apartment "Bobby?" he calls out as he scans the living room and finds Bobby laid out on the couch clutching a bottle of beer and a half eaten cake; but not just any cake, Sunni's favorite cake — the one she always likes to make.

Tony shakes Bobby awake, "Get up!"

Bobby is startled and immediately goes on the defensive trying to hit Tony with the bottle of beer. But Tony grabs his wrist and shakes out of his hand.

"Shit!" Bobby yells as the bottle crashes to the floor and splatters its contents all over his sneakers.

Tony grabs him around the collar, "Where's Sunni?"

Bobby tenses, not prepared for that question. But then he puts on his poker face, "I don't know man; she not at home?"

Tony gives him a rough shake, "When did you last see her and why the fuck is she cooking for you?" Fully awake, Bobby looks around as if he doesn't know where he is; but he's only stalling for time. "She left it by the door, she's a sweet kid," he says, avoiding eye contact.

But Tony's not buying it. "Where is she mutherfucker?!"

"How am I supposed to know? I can't keep up with some teenager!"

Tony releases Bobby's collar with a shove; but he doesn't take his eyes off him. They stare at each other, like in a duel, Bobby sitting, Tony standing. Tony goes over ever little interaction he had with Sunni earlier in the week, including the incident with her dog. He wonders if he drove her away. Maybe she took off with Jin — with the help of Bobby. His upper lip twitches as he pulls out his service revolver. "I'm going to ask you again," he says as he removes the safety and points the barrel at the floor. "When did you last see Sunni and where is she now?"

Bobby stares at the gun and then shifts his gaze to Tony's face. "I don't know man," he says.

Tony points the gun at Bobby's head.

"Whoa! Wait! What the hell?!" Bobby throws his hands up defensively as if they could stop bullets.

"You know everything that happens in this fucking town. You're eating Sunni's food and now you're telling me you don't know where she is? I think you're lying."

Bobby holds out his hands, "You can't just shoot me in cold blood, man."

Tony steadies his weapon and aims it at the center of Bobby's forehead. "Is she with Jin?" he asks.

Bobby stutters out a lie. "I told her to stay away from that kid," he says. "I think h-h-h-he working with Lucky softening them girls up. I ain't got exact proof; but I got good information that it could be true." Lucky is relieved as Tony lowers his weapon, so he decides to add another lie for good measure. "I think she went back to him...I tried to talk her out of it but you know how they are."

Tony frowns at this new piece of information even though he's not sure how much of it is true. He points the gun at Bobby again. "And you never told me this?" he asks.

Bobby shakes his head, "I just found out, just recently." He looks at the gun, "Can you put that way?—Please."

Tony hesitates, then puts the safety back on the gun and shoves it onto his holster. "Where's Jin? And don't tell me you don't know where. You know where he is," Tony says gruffly.

Bobby nods, "I can show you where they hang out." He starts to stand but Tony grabs his wrist again. Unhooking his cuffs from his duty belt, Tony slaps the cuffs on Bobby and leads him out of the apartment.

Cuffed with his hands in front, Bobby discretely fishes out his cell phone from his pants pocket as Tony makes his way from the back passenger side to the driver side door. Bobby sends off a quick text — "The barn on hwy 9" — and tucks the phone under his thigh once Tony gets into the car.

***

Tony parks the police cruiser a hundred feet from the barn and steps into the road. He secures the backdoor and draws his pistol as he creeps through the high grassy area. He goes on high alert as he approaches the barn, his ears perked for even the slightest sound. But there's mostly silence, he hears only the chirping of birds and the wind rustling through the grass. He steps closer to the barn door and keeps his gaze locked on the loft window, but he can't see a soul. He steps carefully up the stairs leading to the barn door, the cracked wood whining under his feet. The door is slightly ajar so he has a limited visual. He thinks he sees someone, but he's not so sure. "Sunni?" he calls out. But there's no response. He readies his weapon as he pulls open the barn door and then there's a loud bang right before he feels the bone in his shoulder shatter. The force of the gunshot sends him flying backwards and tumbling down the stairs. Landing on the hard ground, he lets out a grunt and instinctively reaches for his gun; but his arm isn't working. Before he can sort his thoughts and come to his feet a heavy boot crashes into his shoulder wound sending a fresh wave of pain through him. He lets out a groan as a familiar face comes into view.

"Carlos?" Tony asks, his tone more surprised than angry. He turns his head to find several pairs of police issued boots surrounding him. He's unable to focus well as the pain radiates down his arm.

"Told you to mind your own business, Tony," Carlos says. "You never listen."

Tony sees the baton coming. A sharp pain radiates through his frontal lobe — lights out.

Chapter 18

Sunni sits on the floor in the basement of the abandoned house just off the busy main street. Her knees pressed against her chin, she rocks back and forth. The day before she had only heard Lucky's voice through the basement window, but now she has the displeasure of being his captive. Tony is only a few feet from her corner prison. Sitting between Lucky and Carlos, he's handcuffed to a chair with his arms and ankles bound tight and blood dripping from his shoulder. The Captain sits on a tattered sofa chair with Sunni's satchel at his feet.

"What did you think you were going to do, Tony?" the Captain says as he crosses his right foot over his left thigh and rests his gaze on Tony's battered face.

Tony is barely able to lift his swollen eyelids. But he coughs and struggles to breathe as he looks past the Captain to get a glance of Sunni. She's trying hard to not tremble; but it's no use. She's convinced that she's going to die. And when the Captain looks over his shoulder at her, that belief of imminent death becomes stronger.

"Nothing you can do for her, Tony," the Captain says. "I tried to tell ya' she's nothing but trouble. But you didn't want to listen."

"Never does," Carlos interjects as he taps his bloodstained police baton against his leg. "Was always a hard head to crack," he chuckles.

The Captain nods and comes to his feet. All Tony can see is his belt buckle because he doesn't have the strength to lift his head to look the man in the face.

"I can't have ya' messing up this town, Tony. There's a balance about things here…a real fine balance. It's why things work," the Captain says as he steps closer and peers down at the man. He grabs Tony by the hair and yanks, forcing him to look up. Tony lets out a groan as the back of his neck crackles. He starts to say something, but he can't find the right words. So he lets his intense gaze speak the hatred and deep sense of betrayal he's feeling. He had trusted the man with his life and that of his daughter. And before the truth was revealed, he really believed that the Captain was one of the few good ones.

"You was always an idealist, Tony. Never could get ya' to see how things really worked down here in the dirt with the rest of us," the

Captain says, disdain dripping off his lips. The Captain releases Tony's hair and turns to look at Sunni again. "And so what are we to do with you?"

Sunni keeps her gaze lowered, afraid to look up. But then she hates herself for it. If she's going to die, she figures that she might as well die with a little bit of her dignity intact. She forces herself to look at the Captain, daring to aim her angry gaze right at his eyes. "I'm gonna' kill you," she says to him.

The Captain laughs and turns to look at Lucky. "Call that boy in here," he says.

Lucky nods, "No problem, boss," and sends a quick text message.

Sunni's intense glare widens as she shifts her gaze to the stairs leading up to the basement door. She doesn't even need to see the boy's full frame before she realizes he's Jin. She closes her eyes and a piercing fear overwhelms her. Had he betrayed her? Had he been part of it all along? She doesn't want to know the answers if they'll confirm her fears. The possibility of what they had being a lie makes her welcome death.

Jin stops at the base of the stairs as he catches sight of Sunni. He gives the Captain and Lucky an accusatory look, but he seems unable to take another step forward.

"Come on in here, boy," the Captain says. "This partly yo' mess too."

Jin looks at Sunni just as she is opening her eyes again. And then he looks away, unable to face her. He drags his feet and slowly makes his way towards the Captain.

"I want you to take this here girl and Officer Gavilan out into them woods, since that's where they like to meet and all," the Captain says. "And put a bullet in her head."

Tony weakly struggles with his restraints and finds his own voice. "Don't you fucking touch her," he groans. Jin joins his chorus of dissent, "You want me to kill her?"

"That's what I said," the Captain snaps. "You got a problem with that, boy?"

Jin gives Lucky a pleading look but it's greeted with slight shake of the head.

And against his better judgment Jin speaks up again, "I just think it's a waste of —"

"Did I ask you what you think?" the Captain asks.

"No," Jin answers.

"Then do what I say."

Jin takes a step back, his head tilting down and his gaze resting on the concrete basement floor. He can hear Sunni's quiet whimpers and he can feel her looking at him. He feels like a failure because he's unable to keep his promise.

The Captain motions towards Lucky, "Get the other officers down here. He's gonna' need help getting them into that car."

"Got it boss," Lucky says as he jogs towards the stairs.

The Captain grabs Sunni's satchel and pulls out her dagger. "Bury her with this," he says as he hands Jin the knife.

***

Tony's hands are cuffed tightly behind his back as Carlos and two other cops lead him out of the house. He looks at Carlos through swollen eyes. "Let her go, Carlos. She's just a kid," Tony says, but his protests fall on deaf ears. Sunni follows closely behind them, her hands bound behind her back with zip ties which dig into her wrists. Jin presses his fingers gently into her arm as he guides her down the sidewalk towards a parked car with the trunk popped open. Tony starts to struggle. He's got no intention of going into that trunk without a fight. He musters every ounce of energy he has left to struggle against the three men, but it's to no avail. They easily subdue him and Carlos knocks him unconscious with the butt of his gun.

"Get him in there!" Carlos orders the two cops, and they roll Tony's limp body into the trunk of the car. Sunni's silent tears are joined with deep, sorrowful whimpers as she's guided by Jin to the opening of the trunk.

"Need help with her?" Carlos asks as he holsters his gun.

Jin shakes his head, "No. I got it." And as the three men disperse, he slowly turns Sunni around so that her back is to the trunk and he's standing face to face with her. He looks into her teary eyes, the feeling in his heart matching her sorrow. "I promised ya' I would protect ya'," he says as he reaches behind his back and pulls her dagger from his waistband. "I plan on keeping that promise." He looks around to find that Carlos is sitting in the driver's seat while the other two cops have gone back into the house.

"What's taking you so long?" Carlos yells out.

"Quick, get in the trunk," Jin whispers as he presses the dagger's handle into Sunni's bound hands. She lies down in the trunk, too stunned to even question him. And before she can murmur a thank you, he slams shut the trunk's door and there is darkness.

***

The ride down Hwy 9 is a bumpy one, making it difficult for Sunni to unsheathe her dagger. They hit another pothole. Tony groans and slowly regains consciousness.

"Tony?" Sunni calls out in the darkness of the trunk.

Tony takes a shallow breath, but his voice is weak. "You okay?" he asks.

"I have my knife...he gave me my knife."

"What?"

"I can't get the cover off of it...I need help getting it off."

Tony wiggles his fingers around but can only feel the fabric of Sunni's t-shirt. "You gonna need to inch it off Sunni, take your time."

Sunni slowly begins inching the cover off the blade, but loses her grip when the car hits another pothole. She grasps around for the knife, but she can't feel it. "I don't know...I lost it."

"It's here...stay calm," Tony says. He presses himself to the back wall of the trunk to give Sunni more room. "Get on your back."

Sunni rolls onto her back and immediately feels the dagger under her thigh. "I can feel it," she says as she scoots down so she can grab it. "I think the covers off. "I'm gonna' cut ya' free—"

"No...you can't cut through these metal cuffs," Tony says. "Listen to me...I need you stay calm...try to calm your breathing."

Sunni tries to take a deep breath but can't. "I can't breathe," she says.

"Concentrate, Sunni," Tony says. "I need you to cut through your ties."

"I don't think I can."

"Yes you can...but you can't do it using the handle...grab the blade and cut."

The car comes to a stop and Sunni begins to panic. "I can't—"

"I'm not going to let you die here...you will do it...now!"

Sunni works her fingers down to the blade and begins to saw at the ziptie. Her efforts are making progress but not without slashes to her hand. She lets out a cry of pain.

"Just endure it," Tony says.

Sunni continues to cut at the ziptie until it pops it open.

"Find the latch on the trunk," Tony says. But Sunni searches and finds nothing. "Shhh," Tony says as he hears the car doors open

Sunni stops pushing against the trunk and her heart pounds as she hears Carlos and Jin approaching. She conceals her dagger beneath her bloody hand and forearm. Keys jingle and the trunk pops open. Covered in a sheet of sweat, Sunni trembles as she looks into Carlos' face.

"Be brave," Tony tries to comfort her.

"Out you go," Carlos says as he leans into the trunk to grab Sunni. Sunni looks to Jin, but she catches only a momentary glimpse of him before Carlos' frame obstructs her view.

And as Carlos pulls her from the trunk she flicks her dagger from under her arm and thrusts the blade into his stomach. Carlos lets out a low guttural groan as he releases his grasp on Sunni. Blood oozes from his midsection as she retracts the blade. He stumbles back and goes for his gun, but Jin quickly grabs it and points it at him. Carlos turns to face Jin. "Give me that gun, boy."

Sunni quickly gets out of the trunk and stabs Carlos again, this time in his back. Carlos drops to the ground, but Sunni doesn't let up as her rage bubbles to the surface. She plunges the blade into his neck, his shoulder and anywhere else she can reach. She stabs him repeatedly, not stopping until she is exhausted and he is dead. Covered in blood she stumbles back to the car trunk.

"Run, Sunni," Jin says as he points the gun at her.

Sunni looks over her shoulder at him. Had he not gone through all this trouble to save them? "What are you doing?" she asks.

"You can go, but he can't," Jin says

"Just go," Tony urges her. He tries to lift himself out of the trunk but he doesn't have enough strength.

"We can all go," Sunni says. "We can run away."

Jin shakes his head. "When ya' gonna' stop dreaming? We can't run away…ain't no place to run, Sunni."

Sunni's voice cracks. "So you're going to kill him?" She pulls out her necklace with the ring on it, "Just how Lucky killed them girls — killed Patricia?"

Sunni points her dagger at Jin. "You're going to have to kill me too."

"Sunni!" Tony yells out trying to lift himself again, but with no success.

Jin shoots at the ground near her feet. Sunni jumps back. She wants to believe that Jin would never shoot her, never intentionally harm her. "Just let us go…you can say we got away."

Jin frowns hard. "Why you care so much for him?" He points the gun at Tony and pulls the trigger. "Now you got no reason to stay." Sunni screams as the bullet pierces Tony's skull. "Tony!" He slumps down into the trunk, his wide-eyes looking up at her. She frantically tries to shake him awake, hoping that somehow he can survive. "Please don't leave me! Please!" she cries as the floor of the trunk becomes stained with Tony's blood.

Jin backs away, he had a choice to make and it was Sunni, even if she will never see it that way. He looks at her one last time and takes off running. Sunni continues to shake Tony, trying to wake him, but it useless — he's dead.

***

Sunni sits in the trunk with Tony's dead body laying next to her. She carefully places his hands over his chest and closes his eyes. He seems so peaceful to her. She rests her hand on top of his. "I never told you how much you meant to me," she says. "Or thanked ya' for doing so much for me when nobody…." She chokes on her words as a sob forces its way up. She tries to suppress it. She wants to be the tough girl Tony was trying to make her. She takes a deep breath, beating down the sorrow, burying it deep and replacing it with something more useful — rage. "I just want to let you know that...that this ain't over..." She clutches her dagger, gripping the handle tight. And she lets the anger wash over her. "I promise you...that....that they're gonna' pay for what they did...every last fucking one of them."

###

About The Author

SunHi Mistwalker is a freelance writer who enjoys exploring themes of societal collapse and how the disintegration of a community impacts the individual and family. "New Hope City" is her first full-length novel and the first book in a trilogy. If you enjoyed this book, please leave a review and join this author's mailing list at **www.sunhimistwalker.com** to get notifications on the publication of future books by this author.

Read More Speculative Fiction

By

SunHi Mistwalker

After The Darkness

A post-apocalyptic series that transports you into a frozen future.

Even in a world of never-ending winters and permanent darkness, fourteen-year-old Nadia Comani has everything she could ever want: power, privilege, a loving family and most importantly warmth. But her family's refusal to compromise their values changes everything. Nadia is cast down from her pedestal of power onto the trash heap of the lower classes. No longer guaranteed a life of ease, Nadia faces a future of servitude. Branded as powerless and deviant, will Nadia muster the strength to save herself and what remains of her family?

Get "After The Darkness" at Amazon, Kobo, Nook and other retailers.

Visit **www.sunhimistwalker.com** to receive updates and special deals.

www.ingramcontent.com/pod-product-compliance
Lightning Source LLC
Chambersburg PA
CBHW051245170626
46809CB00004B/1498